# Destiny Binds Us All
## Unique Tales of Fate

## Gary Henicke

Gary Henicke

gary@henickebooks.com

ISBN-13:  978-0615660653 (Gary W. Henicke)

ISBN-10: 0615660657

This book is dedicated to my wife, Jennifer.

# CONTENTS

# THE THERAPIST AND THE PANTHER

Dan Wilson was relieved when he and his wife Deborah passed the last traffic light leading to the freeway. It was only a twenty mile drive and they would be back at their countryside home and away from all the confusion of the city. Dan took off his shoes and looked over at Deborah.

"Thanks for giving me a ride home from work again. I promise that I'll fix my car this weekend. I'll get the water pump Saturday morning and I'll put it on by that afternoon."

Deborah stared at the hood of their Jeep rather than the road.

"I might need some help putting on the new pump. Will ya' help me?"

Again, she seemed lost in thought. Her hands gripped the steering wheel so tightly that her knuckles were white. Dan nudged her.

"Deb? Are you listening to me?"

Deborah looked over at Dan. Her eyes filled up with tears.

"What's the matter, Deb? What's *happened?*"

She would not answer him. As they approached the turnoff to the highway Deborah suddenly veered their Jeep SUV over into the wrong lane and floored the accelerator pedal.

"*Deborah*!" Dan shouted at her. "What the heck are you doing?"

As Dan tried to grab the steering wheel Deborah repeatedly punched at his face. A dump truck barely avoided a head on collision with them by swerving out of the way. Dan finally managed to grab control of the steering wheel and crammed the Jeep into neutral. He then guided the vehicle to the shoulder just before a large group of cars approached horns honking.

Dan moved over and stomped on the brake pedal. He calmly put the Cherokee in park and took the key out of the ignition. Deborah burst into tears.

"What're you trying to do, *kill yourself?*"

She raised her head and looked Dan in the eye.

"*Yes!* Yes, I was trying to kill myself. I'm just sick and tired of living."

Dan sighed heavily. He knew that his wife had been depressed since her mother had died two months earlier, but he had no idea that it would escalate to suicide.

"That does it. I've tried and tried to get you to talk to somebody about this, but you said you'd get over it. Tomorrow I'll take you to a therapist who works in my office building."

Deborah frowned at Dan. She felt betrayed.

"I told you I don't need a therapist. Why don't you just leave me *alone*? She looked down in shame. "You deserve someone better than me."

Dan put his shoes back on and traded places with Deborah. Neither said much to one another until Dan pulled into the garage and shut off the engine.

"I think you should go pet Ebony for awhile," Dan suggested. "You always say that calms you down."

Deborah nodded and then started for Ebony's enclosure.

"I'll get dinner started," Dan called after her.

He watched her walk to the enclosure. He could hear Ebony purring as Deborah knelt down and hugged him. Deborah had Ebony before they met two years ago. The black panther had been a gift from her uncle. Ebony was one of the main reasons Dan and Deborah moved onto their ranchette after they married. Deborah had to apply for a special permit to keep the panther, agreeing to regular inspections.

Dan made supper, but frequently checked on Deborah to see if she was alright. She came inside the house at sunset.

"Feeling better?" Dan asked as he sat down to dinner.

"I don't know. I guess so," Deborah mumbled.

She headed straight for the sofa and flopped down on it face first.

"Hey, I made your favorite- *fried chicken.*" Dan looked into the den at her for a response, but there was none. "Well, if you get hungry, it's here." Dan took his iced tea into the den and sat down on the coffee table in front of Deborah. "Do you still love me?"

Deborah sat up and frowned.

"Of course I do. I told you it's me. I *hate* myself."

"Why did you try to kill yourself by having a head-on collision? You could have killed someone else at the same time."

Deborah stared right through Dan.

"Yeah I know," Deborah said. "You don't know what it's like. Both of your parents are still alive. I'm all mixed up right now." Deborah snapped out of her trance-like state. "I could have killed *you* too. I'm so sorry."

She hugged him. Dan stroked the back of her head.

"Look, I'm grateful that nobody got hurt. You're alive and you're gonna get better because you're going to get help." Dan pulled out his wallet and leafed through his business cards. "Let's see; here it is. She's on the seventh floor. *Liz Fullwood-Schneider, Women's Therapy.*" He handed the card to Deborah. "I got the lady's card after your mother passed. I kept hoping you would get better. Barbara, the receptionist at work, went to her when her husband divorced her. She says the therapist really helped get her life in order. She told me she's never been happier."

Deb looked at the card and gave a tight smile.

"What harm can it do? Things can't get much worse for me than they are right now."

Dan gave Deborah a kiss on the cheek.

"I'll see if Barbara can get you in early since it's urgent."

Deborah had a difficult time sleeping that night. When she did sleep she tossed and turned as if in agony. Dan suspected that she was dreaming about the suicide attempt. Dan did not want to fall asleep himself for fear that Deborah might make another suicide attempt while he was sleeping. He still felt guilty about his wife's depression. He thought he was a failure as a husband for not pulling Deborah out of her depression after her mother's death. He chastised himself for not taking Deborah to the hospital immediately after the incident on the highway.

Dan found Deborah in the kitchen the next morning. She was dressed and was staring at a notepad. Deborah gave Dan a tight smile and handed the notepad to him. She had written *For the Therapist* at the top of the page. Deborah had written a timeline of sorts beginning with her mother's death from a heart attack. She included a list of the things she had lost interest in such as her job as a nurse, her friends and love of food. Near the end of the list she had underlined *Tried to kill myself and the man I love.* She circled her last item simply stating, *I am empty.*

Dan and Deborah left early so they could set up the emergency appointment. They waited in the parking lot for Dan's coworker. A few minutes later, Barbara pulled into the space next to them.

Dan and Deborah got out of their Jeep and walked over to her car.

"Morning, Dan. Is this your wife?"

"Yeah, this is Deb."

Deborah shook hands with the receptionist.

"Hi, I'm Barbara. I work with Dan."

Deborah nodded. "I recognize your voice from the times I've called Dan at work."

"Listen, Barbara, Deb is having some problems and needs to get an appointment with that therapist you told me about. Remember I got her business card from you?"

"You mean Liz?"

"Yeah, that's the one. Could you ask her if she could talk with Deb right away? It's really urgent."

Barbara looked around the parking lot.

"There's her car over there. Let's go up to the office and call her. I'm sure she can do it."

The three of them rode up in the elevator to the twelfth floor that housed the offices of the insurance agency Dan and Barbara worked for. Barbara put on her headset and dialed the therapist's office. The call took no longer than a minute before the therapist agreed to see Deborah.

"Well, it's all set," Barbara said. "Liz said you can go down right now if you like."

Dan smiled and looked at Deborah.

"You want me to go with you?"

Deborah grabbed his hand.

"You'd better. This was your idea, you know."

As Dan and Deborah rode the elevator down to the seventh floor, Deborah fidgeted about. She took out her list and folded and refolded the paper. The idea of telling a complete stranger the most intimate details of one's personal problems even made Dan feel a bit uncomfortable.

The therapist's office was located at the end of the hall. Most of the other offices were not even open yet so the hallways seemed somewhat ominous. Dan opened the door and let Deborah walk into the waiting room first. Most of the lights in the waiting room were turned off. The counter where the receptionist would be was empty. Beside the counter was a door with a large international symbol of a man on it just like on doors to public restrooms. The sign was encircled and had a slash through it, evidently meaning, "No men allowed".

Dan was about to comment on the sign when a woman opened the door and stepped into the room.

"Are you Deborah Wilson?" she asked.

"Yes. I hope this isn't an inconvenience to you," Deborah apologized as she shook the woman's hand.

Gary Henicke

"No, of course not. I don't have any appointments until ten this morning." She opened the door and gestured for Deborah to join her. Deborah took Dan's hand and gave it a gentle tug to let him know she wanted him to join her. The therapist stepped forward and prevented Dan from entering the doorway.

"I'm afraid he can't come in with us. In fact, it's better if he waits outside in the hallway."

Deborah gave Dan a look of perplexion, but he gave her a reassuring nod. Dan turned and walked out into the hallway.

"Wait outside in the hall?" Dan asked himself silently. "What am I a dog or something?" Dan walked back to the elevators. "She just better do a good job; that's all I've got to say."

Barbara was already answering calls when he stepped back into the office. Dan waited for her to finish the phone call before talking with her. She had an embarrassed look upon her face. Evidently, she knew what Dan was going to say. Barbara quickly removed her headset after the call.

"I'm sorry Dan. I forgot to tell you not to go down there. Liz listens to a lot of women going through divorces or abusive relationships. The last thing she wants in her waiting room is a *man*."

"Hey, I understand all that," Dan said trying to keep from being offended. "Deborah is my wife for crying out loud. I'm not some wife-beater or adulterer."

Barbara shrugged her shoulders and put her headset back on to answer another call. Dan started for his office.

"Good grief, a lot of us really *do* care about our wives. What are they gonna do next; bar us from the delivery room?"

Dan had been working for quite some time before he realized that it was already 10:30.

"The therapist said she had an appointment at ten. Why hasn't Deb come by to tell me how it went?" Dan asked himself silently.

He almost picked up the phone to call down to the therapist's office, but suddenly remembered the "no men allowed" sign on the door. Instead, Dan called Barbara and had her call the office. Dan was surprised to learn that Deborah was still talking with the therapist.

Dan took his lunch break at eleven thirty. He rode the elevator down to the seventh floor and noticed Deborah coming down the hallway.

She rushed up to Dan, hugged him tightly and then kissed him.

"Hey there, did you finish talking with the therapist?"

"Yep. Kinda long, huh?"

"I'd say four hours is kinda long." Dan could see a tremendous change in her eyes. She had not been this happy in months. "What happened in there?"

Deborah stepped into the elevator.

"Let's just say she turned on the lights in what had been a very dark room."

Dan thought about that answer for a second before the elevator doors started to close.

"Come on and get in. You can buy me lunch."

Deborah was doing so much better that Dan agreed to let her drive home by herself after they had lunch. It had been the therapist's suggestion as a way for Dan to show his trust.

Dan was relieved to see Deborah waiting for him in the parking lot when he got off work. He had been worrying throughout the afternoon and had great difficulty concentrating on his work. Dan noticed Deborah was still smiling and was in the same mood as she was when she left the therapist's office. Dan walked up to the driver's side of the Cherokee expecting Deborah to move over to the passenger side.

"Hey buddy, I'm drivin' this thing today. Just hop in the other side and let me do all the work."

Dan paused for a second and then remembered how the therapist wanted him to show his trust. He thought he might be tempting fate, but walked around to the passenger side and slid into the bucket seat. He strapped on his seat belt and silently prayed that Deborah was not faking a good mood. Needless to say, the drive home was pleasant with no incidents like the day before.

It had been two weeks since Deborah's suicide attempt and she still seemed happier than ever. The therapist told Deborah that they were making remarkable progress and so she increased the sessions to three times a week. Deborah never revealed much about what she and Ms. Fullwood-Schneider discussed during their sessions. About all Dan could learn from Deborah was that they talked about him a lot. This revelation made him even more curious. The therapy was outrageously expensive, but Dan could not complain since Deborah seemed to have turned her life around.

Apparently, Deborah got along rather well with, "Liz", as she called her. The two had a great deal in common. They had graduated from the same university, liked the same music, and Liz even had a relative who kept exotic cats. Liz once told Deborah that she also planned to move to the country so she could raise a lion or a tiger.

Ebony was Deborah's pride and joy so Dan suspected that the two spent much of the therapy sessions talking about jungle cats. Dan knew that, above all, Deborah needed a friend to talk with. None of her friends cared much for her pet panther. Ebony was hostile towards them, so like Dan, they could not share in the pleasure she got from being with the big cat.

Most Saturday afternoon's Deborah and Dan spent time together working around the house. Just as they were preparing to work on Dan's car, Liz called. Liz and Deborah spent the better part of four hours on the phone. Dan did not want to eavesdrop on the conversation so he decided to go into the city to kill some time. He noticed that the movie Deborah had been dying to see was playing at their favorite theater. He decided to make reservations at the best restaurant in the city to reward Deborah for her efforts. Deborah was excited about the idea and suggested that they dress up for the occasion. Deborah told Dan she had a surprise for him which she would reveal at dinner.

Just as they were backing the Jeep out of the garage, Ms. Liz Fullwood-Schneider drove up.

"Hey look! It's *Liz*," Deb yelled as she ran out to the driveway.

Dan could not believe Liz's timing or Deborah's reaction. Even though they spent twelve hours together during the week and four hours earlier on the phone; Deborah acted as though she had not seen her in weeks. It was kind of pathetic the way Deborah went out of her way to make her feel welcome. She ushered Liz into the house with neither of them saying a word to Dan as they brushed past him.

"Well heck, I guess we're not going out tonight are we honey?" Dan muttered to himself.

Dan went back into the house to take off his jacket and tie. He could hear Deborah and Liz having a lively conversation in the living room. They were laughing and carrying on like a couple of old friends who had not seen each other in years. Suddenly, the talking stopped and then the front door shut.

"Do you still want to go out?" Dan called out from in the bedroom. "I can call the restaurant and I think we can catch a later showing of that movie you want see." Dan heard no response so he went into the living room. "Hey, did you hear me? Deb?" He opened the front door and saw Liz's car speeding away with Deborah in the passenger seat. Dan shook his head. "Now that's cold. Cold-blooded, man."

Rather than mope around the house, Dan decided to get a burger and visit one of his friends. He left a note for Deborah in case she got back before he did.

Dan visited his childhood friend Jerry. Jerry had gotten married in college and he and his wife had two children, ages eight and two. Dan was a bit envious of Jerry since he had kids. Deborah was not sure if she was ready for children, but Dan was. He thought about being a father just about every day now.

Dan did not say anything to Jerry or his wife about Deborah's suicide attempt or her therapy. He really wanted to put it out of his mind. Needless to say, he now began to have second thoughts about Deborah's therapist. He thought it was strange for a therapist to carry on a friendship with a current client. If her therapy was completed then he could understand, but Liz kept telling Deborah she had a long way to go. The whole matter seemed unprofessional.

Dan got home around ten thirty that night. Deborah was still gone. He watched television for a couple of hours or so then went to bed around one in the morning. Dan was beginning to worry about Deborah. She had forgotten to take her phone. He had no way to contact Liz because her cell number was not listed on her business card. Dan just laid there and tried to convince himself that Deborah would explain her actions when she got home.

Deborah finally made it home around three thirty in the morning. Dan awakened as soon as he heard the car door slam outside. He watched Deborah walk unsteadily to the edge of the bed to take off her shoes. There was a faint smell of alcohol. He faked a cough hoping Deborah would explain her actions. She just turned and looked at him. Dan figured that she would not give an explanation on her own so he gave her an opportunity to do so.

"Where did you two go?" he asked her.

"We went to the movies and to a couple of bars."

Deborah continued to undress.

"You know, I wouldn't have minded if you had invited Liz to go to dinner and the movie with us."

"Yeah, so?"

"So, it would have been better than just ignoring me. That was kind of cold-blooded."

She stood up and faced him.

"Cold-blooded huh? And you've never been cold-blooded to me?"

"Well I probably have been, but not intentionally. Besides, I would have at least explained myself. We had plans tonight and you and Liz just took off and didn't even bother to tell me anything."

Deborah crawled into bed. She stayed near the edge with her back towards Dan.

"You know, Liz said you'd be upset. She was right. You do think of me as your teenage daughter. I broke my curfew and didn't tell my daddy where I was going."

Dan could not believe what he was hearing.

"That's overanalyzing the situation. This isn't a question of power; it's just a matter of common courtesy."

Deborah pretended not to hear him. Dan rolled over and let the matter go.

Dan had all but forgotten the incident by morning. After breakfast he got dressed for church. Dan noticed that Deborah had not dressed yet. He found her in the den reading the newspaper.

"Aren't you coming to church?" he asked.

"Nope," she said as she continued to read the paper.

"You've hardly missed a Sunday since we got married. Do you feel bad or something?"

She put the newspaper down and looked at Dan.

"I'm not *hung-over* if that's what you're trying to say. I just don't want to go is all. I don't care for the preacher there."

"Aw, he's alright. He's real old-fashioned and all, but at least he doesn't yell and preach that fire and brimstone stuff."

Deborah returned to her newspaper.

Dan went to church alone. It was strange not having his wife sitting next to him. It was Deborah who had convinced Dan to go to church with her every Sunday. Dan explained to his church friends that Deborah was at home because she was ill.

Dan brought home some Chinese food for lunch. Deborah was on the phone. As he expected, she was talking to Liz. She spoke very softly whenever Dan was near her. A few minutes later she finished her phone call and joined Dan at the table.

"Liz says I should go back to work," Deborah said as she spooned some garlic chicken onto a plate.

"Yeah? Well, I think that's a great idea. I knew they couldn't do without a R.N. at the doctor's office. Dr. Morgan was kind to let you take an extended leave of absence after your mother passed."

"Oh, I'm gonna quit that job."

"*Quit?*" Dan put his fork down. "But that's a good job. They didn't have to keep your job open. That was very kind of them. Besides, the hours are the same as mine and you've always said you wanted to stay there as long as you could."

"Yeah, well Liz thinks I need a change. She says she can get me a job in the psychiatric hospital. I'd be working from three to midnight."

Dan frowned.

"Aw, Deb. We'd hardly see each other. I'd be asleep by the time you came home and..."

"*And* I wouldn't be here to make your supper, right? You'll just have to cook for yourself. This is my life and my decision. You don't have any right to tell me when and where I can work."

Again, Dan thought Deborah was overanalyzing the situation, but he decided not to tell her that.

"I'm not telling you anything. I just want to see you as much as possible. Excuse me for being selfish."

After lunch Dan began watching a ballgame in the bedroom. He heard a car drive up and he instinctively knew it was Liz. Nearly every phone call was from Liz and now it seemed she was going to visit Deborah every chance she got.

Dan noticed Deborah and Liz heading over to Ebony's cage. Dan quickly got up and went to a window that would give him a perfect view of the enclosure. Ebony was especially hostile to strangers and Dan wanted to see Liz jump back when Ebony snapped at her. Ebony was already pressed against the chain link fence when Liz and

Deborah walked up to the enclosure. Liz knelt down in front of Ebony and extended her hand.

"You nut; he's gonna bite..."

Dan interrupted himself when Ebony sniffed Liz's hand, yawned and then rolled over on his back.

"Aw, *come on*! What are you a cocker spaniel?"

Dan went back to his ballgame.

"Man, I've been trying to pet that panther for over two years now. He probably would have bitten my finger off if I had stuck my hand in his face."

When Dan came home for work the next day he found Deborah rummaging through a closet. She had her tennis racquet, bowling ball, and a pair of skis on the floor.

"You planning a big sports weekend for us?" Dan asked.

"No. Liz told me to get rid of this stuff. She has a friend who could use it."

Dan thought Deborah was kidding at first.

"Are you serious? Deb, you're the one who got me to play tennis with you." He picked up one of the skis. "We just bought these skis. We've had a lot of fun doing all these sports together. We've always played tennis or bowled together on the weekends. It's not like you don't use these things."

"Hey, I'm sorry, but Liz says they're harmful."

"*Harmful?* How can playing tennis be harmful for crying out loud? It's good exercise."

"Liz says that I should stop because you always beat me at sports."

"I thought we always played for fun? Heck, most of the time we never even kept score." Dan shook his head. "I think Liz is wrong on this one."

"Liz said you'd be against it. She says you like to play sports with me because it gives you another aspect of domination."

Dan sighed heavily and plopped down on the sofa.

"Yep, that's right. I just love to run your life. That's why I *made* you quit your nursing job the day after we married. That's why I *forced* you to stay home and have babies. That's why I *made* you sell Ebony to the zoo so I could have a pen to keep my huntin' dogs. I just love to order you around." Dan looked up at Deborah. "Don't you see how ridiculous this all sounds? That therapist thinks I'm some sort of evil, conniving, wife-beater. Why don't you set her straight and stand up for me?"

Deborah said nothing. She started collecting the sports equipment.

"I had an interview today at the psychiatric hospital," she said. "I start work in two days."

Dan nodded in appreciation. He was glad that Deborah would be working again. He hoped the work would help keep her mind off of any depression she might still have. He also hoped her relationship with Liz would be ending soon.

Three weeks passed and Deborah was still seeing Liz three times a week. Liz and Deborah spent time together on Deb's days off. The only time Dan saw Deborah was for a few hours on the weekends. Deborah now slept in the guest bedroom because she said she did not feel comfortable sleeping with Dan. Just before leaving for work, Dan would often peek in on Deborah as she slept.

Dan and Deborah's marriage was continually deteriorating. Deborah hardly spoke to Dan when they were in the same room. Liz had never even spoken to Dan since he first met her. Dan managed to drag some more information out of Deborah about her therapy sessions with Liz. As he suspected, Deborah admitted that Liz believed that Dan was a major cause of her depression. According to Liz, Deborah's suicide attempt with Dan in the car might actually have been an unintentional murder attempt. Dan pleaded with Deborah to change therapists, but she insisted on staying with Liz.

Dan knew that Liz despised him mainly because she had not taken the time to get to know him. He decided to try and get to know Liz. Dan tried several times to make appointments at her office, but Liz refused to see him. The next time Liz came by the house Dan said hello to her and tried to engage a conversation with her about Ebony. Dan felt extremely awkward when she stared at him and said nothing. It was like talking to someone who could not understand English.

Not only was Liz Deborah's new best friend, but now even Ebony adored her. Dan could not believe it when he saw Liz sitting in Ebony's enclosure stroking his back. Nobody but Deborah and her uncle had been able to go into the cage. Dan still had the scars on his leg when Ebony took a swipe at him two years ago. Dan had repeatedly warned Deborah to get Ebony declawed, but she felt that would be too cruel.

Dan was still having problems with his old car and decided to spend a Saturday afternoon putting on a new carburetor. Deborah had the day off and was tending to Ebony. It was already one thirty and Liz had not even called. Things were beginning to seem like old times before Dan noticed Liz's car coming down the road.

"Here comes Liz again," Dan said while pointing to the direction of the approaching car. "What have you two got planned today?"

Deb closed the gate to Ebony's enclosure.

"Liz wants to teach Ebony to hunt."

Dan nodded and said nothing more. This was the nicest Deborah had been to him in several days. Lately, he felt like he was walking on eggshells around Deborah. She often snapped at him for no reason. All his questions were met with overreaction or extreme suspicion.

Liz parked her car directly behind Dan's. If he got his car running he would not be able to back out of the driveway if he wanted to.

Every one of Liz's visits was started with the same ritual. Liz and Deborah hugged and acted as if they had not seen each other in years. The whole greeting ritual was so pathetic that Dan could hardly stand to be around when Liz came over.

Liz went around to the trunk and took out a large crate full of rabbits.

"Oh, jeez," Dan said under his breath as he realized Liz's intentions.

"Hey, you two aren't really going to let Ebony kill those rabbits are you?"

His question was met with only cold silence and blank stares.

Deborah went inside the enclosure to put Ebony on a long leash. As soon as he was outside the enclosure he strained to get at the crate of rabbits Liz had set on the ground. Liz reached into a leather bag she had on her shoulder and took out a pump spray bottle.

"What's the spray for?" Deborah asked her.

"This is deer musk spray," Liz said as she coated the struggling rabbit. "Ebony will learn to associate the scent with hunting. The musk spray signals the cat to do two things: hunt and then kill."

Liz nodded for Deborah to release Ebony.

"Aw, please don't let Ebony off his leash, Deb. It's too dangerous what with all the kids who play down by the river."

Liz turned and gave Dan a dirty look. "Why don't you go back to pretending to fix your car and stop trying to control Deb's life?"

"Hey, I'm just trying to do what's right. If that cat runs off and hurts somebody we're gonna get sued."

Deb unhooked the leash from Ebony's collar and held him by the back of his neck. He was growling and hissing at the rabbit Liz held in her hand.

"You just leave us alone," Deborah said. "Ebony's not going to run off; he's too interested in the hunt."

Dan slammed the hood of his car and began walking towards the back door.

"Don't worry, I'm outta here. I don't want to see this anyway."

Dan had seen rabbits being hunted by wolves and cougars before on television. The rabbits never made a sound until the end of the chase when they let out a haunting squeal just before they were killed. Dan did not want to be around to hear those squeals. He went into the house and put on some headphones and listened to music.

It did not take Ebony long to kill all the rabbits Liz had brought. Deborah was especially invigorated from the hunting session. Liz decided to incorporate the hunting and killing training into Deborah's overall therapy. Deborah was so excited that she told Dan all about it.

"Yeah, it was great. Liz really knows a lot about big cats. I've never seen Ebony get so aggressive. It had to be that musk spray she had."

Dan realized this was important to Deborah so he tried not to voice any negative opinions.

"I can see where it would be good exercise for Ebony, but what's it supposed to do for you? I mean how long does Liz want you to do this and are you gonna have to buy rabbits every week?"

"Don't you get it?" Deborah asked. "I'm under a lot of stress here and training Ebony to hunt will relieve all that."

Dan failed to understand the logic.

"O.K., I can understand how Liz wants you to relieve stress by doing some kind of activity, so why can't you play tennis with me anymore? You can take out all of your frustrations on the tennis ball."

Deborah was visibly angered. She frowned at Dan and left the room.

Dan was not too surprised when he drove home from work the following Monday and found a pen full of rabbits sitting next to Ebony's enclosure. Ebony was clawing at the chain link fence trying to get at the rabbits so Dan moved the pen to the other side of the garage. He could not get over the fact that Deborah actually planned to let Ebony kill them all. Before she met Liz, Deborah hated to see any animal get hurt, much less killed. She was steadily becoming more and more hard-hearted.

Each day Dan came home from work he noticed one less rabbit in the cage. There were bits of white fur scattered about the lawn and even on Ebony. Liz was obviously helping out Deborah every day because Dan could still smell her peculiar perfume in the house.

Dan had managed to get somewhat used to the rabbit hunting after a week, but nothing prepared him for what he found in Ebony's cage. He had noticed the rabbits' cage was gone as soon as he pulled into the garage. He looked around the yard, but could not find it. As he walked in front of Ebony's enclosure, he noticed a bundle in the corner. Dan's blood pressure rose dramatically when he recognized just what it was. Deborah and Liz had gotten a training dummy shaped like a man and had put Dan's clothes on it. Ebony had ripped the thing to shreds. Dan decided he had had enough and drove straight to the hospital. Teaching Ebony to kill rabbits was one thing, but teaching him to attack human targets was beyond anything rational.

Deborah was in the lab with a co-worker when Dan arrived at the hospital. He waited out in the hallway until Deborah was alone so as not to embarrass her in front of anyone. After the lab technician left he walked calmly into the lab.

"*Dan?* What are you doing here? You're not supposed to be in here."

Dan sat down next to her. He took a deep breath and promised himself he'd remain calm.

"I saw the training dummy in Ebony's cage. You *know* I still wear those clothes you two put on it."

Deborah pushed aside the paperwork she was looking at.

"You *two?* What's that supposed to mean? How do you know it was only me?"

"Aw, come on. I know Liz was there. I smell her perfume in the house every time I come home from work." Again, Dan caught himself and calmed his tone of voice. "This ain't right. You can't train that cat to attack people."

"Why not? People train guard dogs to do the same thing."

"What're you gonna do, let Ebony out to patrol the grounds? That cat is not disciplined enough to know when to stop. He's gonna attack until he kills. What if some kid comes by the house selling candy for school? What if it's the meter reader, or one of our friends? Shoot, that cat could want to kill me."

Deborah's eyes began to fill with tears. It had been the only emotion, other than anger, Deborah had displayed towards Dan in a month. Dan felt that he had finally made some sense to Deborah. She put her face in her hands and sighed.

"I can't stand this anymore. When are you going to stop trying to control every little detail of my life?"

Dan's heart sank. He thought he had gotten through to Deborah, but it was the same overreaction again.

"You can't stand to see Liz and I have a good time, can you?"

"If you call training a panther to kill people a good time than no. *Heck no.*"

Deborah shook her head and stood up.

"I can't talk with you anymore. Just, just get out of here. You're not supposed to be here."

Deborah started to walk out through another door.

"Please promise to stop this nonsense with Ebony," Dan pleaded.

She did not answer. Dan walked slowly out of the hospital to his car. Dan knew in his heart that something terrible had just happened to his marriage. He had tried and tried to be supportive and understanding, but Deborah was becoming someone else.

It was now over one month since Deborah started her therapy with Liz. In those few weeks Deborah had completely changed her philosophy, religion, and politics to mirror those of Liz. She frequently spouted the same radical, man-hating ideology as Liz. She was now completely paranoid of men, especially Dan. None of Deborah's old friends bothered to call or visit because they were turned off by the new Deborah. Dan now realized that he had lost all influence over Deborah. He strongly suspected that Deborah would divorce him any day now.

Dan had tried to find out as much as he could about Liz, but he had little success. Liz was still fairly new in town and most of the other therapists knew nothing about her. Barbara, the receptionist at Dan's workplace only knew that Liz was divorced and had few friends. Barbara did not know if Liz spent so much personal time with her other clients. Liz was now spending the night frequently on Deborah's days off and on the weekends.

Dan felt ashamed to admit to his friends and family that he and Deborah were having serious marital problems. Dan had to tell his sister and family not to come for a planned visit because Deborah refused to give up her and Liz's bedrooms for that particular weekend. Dan even tried to ask Liz to help him with his marriage, but again, he was met with silence. Dan started seeing a marriage counselor twice a week during his lunch hour. He tried to get Deborah to meet with the counselor, but she flatly refused.

One day after Dan came home from work he heard Deborah crying in her bedroom. Not knowing what happened, he knocked on the door to see if she was alright.

"Deb? What's the matter?"

There was no answer so he knocked again.

"Go away!"

It was Liz's voice. Her car was not in the driveway, but she was in there with Deborah.

"What's wrong with Deb?" Dan tried the doorknob, but it was locked.

"Can't I come in and talk with my own wife?"

"No! She's just sick that's all. Just go away and leave us alone."

Something had definitely gone wrong in Deborah's life. She had never let any illness get the best of her, and crying just went against her new, tough personality.

Deborah's dependence on Liz sickened Dan. Liz had drummed the idea into Deborah's thoughts that Dan had been controlling her life, when in fact it was Liz, who was the controller. Dan thought that good therapists were supposed to help their clients become self confident enough to deal with problems on their own. Liz was like a parasite which fed off the power of control. Deborah was so dependent on Liz for everything that she had become much like an addict.

It was Saturday morning and Dan was awakened by Ebony's roars outside his bedroom window. Liz and Deborah were training Ebony again. The cat had gotten so aggressive that Dan couldn't go near the enclosure without Ebony tearing at the fence in an attempt to attack him.

In the past, Dan would have spent the day with Deborah, but those days were long gone. Now, he either spent his time alone or with Jerry and his family. Dan decided to work on his car after breakfast. The car was stalling at stop lights so he wanted to try and fix the problem before he had an accident. When he was ready, Dan looked out the window to make sure that Ebony was in his enclosure. Ebony was in the pen and Liz and Deborah were picking up the remains of whatever Ebony had just mauled beyond recognition.

Just as Dan walked out into the garage he heard his name. Liz and Deborah were evidently having a discussion about him. Dan let his curiosity rule out over his manners and decided to listen in. He was glad he did. Deborah was explaining her reasons for marrying Dan. Judging by the tone of her voice Dan surmised that she thought she had made a big mistake.

"Look Debbie," he heard Liz say. "It's like I told you before about this type of man. He's the church-going, conservative who's polite on the surface, but believe me, Dan is the root of your depression. He's evil."

Dan suspected that Liz had been filling Deborah's head with such nonsense, but he had no idea it was this bad.

Liz continued. "He's the typical type of man that will cheat on you, beat on you, and molest your daughters."

Dan slammed the door leading to the garage. He knew right then that he had to get Liz investigated. He was not sure how he was going to do it, but come Monday morning, he would find out whom to contact. Dan could barely control his anger. He wished he could get an audio recording of Liz so he could back up his charges. He noticed Liz peer around the corner of the house into the garage. Dan hoped that she would be satisfied that he had not heard any of her conversation with Deborah.

Dan whistled and acted like nothing was wrong. He backed his car out onto the driveway where there was more light. He popped open the hood and then went into the house for his toolbox. When Dan came back out he noticed Liz had just leaned into his car to get, or put, something inside it. He looked at Liz, but she had nothing in her hands. Dan peered through the windshield, but saw nothing.

Deborah and Liz stood nearby and looked at Ebony through the chain link fence. Liz suggested that Deborah start keeping Ebony in the house. Dan could not help but let out a snicker at such a suggestion. Liz gave Dan a dirty look and he returned it with one of his own.

"That cat would tear the sofa and the beds to pieces."

Liz started walking towards Dan.

"The way you two have taught Ebony to rip those stuffed mannequins would make it crazy to keep him in the house." Dan leaned over his engine again and started to take off the air cleaner. "Besides, I live in that house too, you know.

By now Liz was three feet from Dan.

"Why don't you just butt out for once," Liz warned. "Everything Debbie wants, you have to butt in and tell her no. You're just a control freak."

Dan had been hoping to debate Liz about control and now was his chance.

"If anybody is a control freak it's *you*. Heck, *Deb* could make up her own mind before she met you. Now she can't even decide what clothes to put on without asking you first. You've got her all bitter towards me and every man on the planet."

Liz laughed loudly. She had a wild look in her eyes.

"Yeah, that's right mister. She's bitter because she trusted you and now she knows the truth about men like you."

Dan shut the hood of his car.

"What about it? What's the truth about me, Ms. Fullwood-Schnieder?"

Liz said nothing, but her face was flushed and she began breathing more heavily. Dan continued.

"Well, what's the truth? Could it be that perhaps I'm *evil*?"

"You *are* evil," Liz said. She actually believed it. She smiled. "You're evil and that's why Debbie's gonna divorce you."

Now Dan was boiling over again with anger. He looked over at Deborah.

"Is that true, Deb?" Deborah turned away and would not answer him. "Look Liz, I've tried to talk to you so we can get these problems fixed. That's why *I* brought Deb to your office." Dan paused for a second. He thought that now he was actually beginning to reason with Liz. "I know I'm not this great husband. That's why I'm seeing a marriage counselor myself. My marriage counselor will tell you that I have some problems, but she'll also tell you that I'm not evil."

"You voted for that *Republican* in that last election."

Liz's comment went right over Dan's head.

"Yeah?" Dan said cautiously. "I don't understand what that has to do with anything."

"Oh, it has everything to do with what you are. You're a neo-Nazi."

Dan was stunned. He turned and laughed loudly.

"Let me understand this. I'm a neo-Nazi because I voted for a Republican?"

Liz nodded. Dan felt his laughter was making her angry.

"Good God, he won all but one county. He got something like sixty-seven per cent of the vote. Are sixty-seven per cent of the people in our state neo-Nazis?"

"*You're* a Nazi," Liz answered coldly. "You're a Nazi for not feeling guilty over a vote like that."

Dan finally realized that it would be impossible to reason with Liz. He now knew just how demented she was.

Liz glanced over at Deborah. She was staring at her feet.

"It would be a crime for someone like you to father a child. You ought to be castrated." Liz again looked at Deborah. "That's why I took Deb to the reproduction clinic yesterday while *you* were at work," Liz admitted with a sinister grin.

Dan quickly walked over to Deborah. She started to cry.

"Deborah? Please tell me she's lying."

Deborah continued to cry. She had aborted their first child. Dan could hear Liz snickering. In a rage he walked over to her and shoved her down onto the concrete driveway. Dan ran into the house and paced around a bit. He knew that he had to get away and think so he grabbed his wallet.

He thought he might take a long drive to calm down and think.

Liz and Deborah were standing near the enclosure as Dan exited the garage. They ignored him as he walked up to his car. The car doors were now locked and the keys were missing from the ignition. Evidently, Liz intended on retaliating against him for pushing her down. Dan walked over to Liz and Deborah.

"O.K., somebody hand over my car keys."

Liz pulled the keys out of her pocket and tossed them into Ebony's enclosure.

"Come on, I just want to go get a part for my car."

"Liz pretended to get the keys, but Dan could see her demented plan in her eyes. She was going to let Ebony out on him for pushing her down. The car keys were near the edge of the fence so Dan quickly reached his fingers through the holes in the fence while Ebony was not looking. The keys were less than an inch out of reach. Just as Dan turned to see if Liz was going to unlock the gate, he was sprayed in the eyes with musk spray. Dan was temporarily blinded by the spray. His vision cleared to a blur and he stumbled around in agony trying to find some sort of weapon. Dan could hear the garage door shut and lock so he knew he could not get back inside the house. Dan took off his shirt and desperately tried to rub the spray out of his eyes so he could find where the water hose was. Just then, Dan heard a very familiar sound. It was the gate to Ebony's enclosure being opened. Dan looked around and saw a blurry figure standing next to the garage.

"Deb! Please don't let her do this!" he pleaded. She just stood there motionless. "*Deb*!"

Dan started running as fast as he could. His plan was to make it to the river that ran by his property. He figured that Ebony would be afraid of the water. Once in the river, he could wash off the musk spray and wade downstream to the neighbor's house for help.

Dan could hear Ebony growling behind him. He was loose and gaining on him. Dan once again wiped his face with his shirt and threw it to the ground. Ebony stopped and began mauling the musk-coated shirt. Dan could barely make out the river just ahead. Ebony once again resumed the chase. Dan tried to evade Ebony, but a human is no match for a full grown panther. The big cat tackled Dan near a large oak tree just on the bank of the river. Dan tried to scramble up the trunk, but the panther sunk its claws around his waist and hauled him down. Dan tried to fend off the panther by wildly swinging his fists and kicking at it. With the musk spray still stinging his eyes, Dan could only see a dark blur. It was only seconds before Ebony began ripping at his face and throat. Dan was a strong and agile man, but he had no chance against the well-trained panther. Dan had been covered with the musk spray and the panther did its job well. It hunted and then it killed.

## PAUL VS. JACK

Paul Benton sighed heavily as he wheeled his lawn mower out of the garage. He looked over his front lawn to make sure there were no obstacles to move. After seven frustrating cranks he finally got the mower started and he began his normal Saturday drudgery.

"Man, I'm sick and tired of wasting my Saturdays with these stupid yard chores." Paul thought for a moment. "I think I'll rip out the lawn and just have a green parking lot for a yard."

It did not take but two minutes before sweat started streaming down Paul's face. He looked around his neighborhood to see if anyone else was crazy enough to be out mowing in the ninety degree heat. Just then he noticed an old van had pulled up to the Henderson's house across the street. Paul watched as a long haired man climbed out and began unloading a lawn mower and gardening tools.

"I guess the Henderson's have gotten tired of doing it themselves," Paul thought.

Paul was now becoming energized by the Henderson's surrender to their outdoor chores. Paul leaned into his mower to help it move along faster. The scruffy gardener's mower was old and not self-propelled like Paul's, but he began to catch up to him. It was amazing to see how fast he could mow with an ordinary push mower. This was a race now. Paul pushed even harder.

The gardener was still mowing the Henderson's front lawn when Paul steered his mower into his backyard. Paul was gasping for air and was soaking wet from the heat, but he did not care. All he wanted to do was prove that he was faster than any gardener.

After finishing his last strip of unmowed lawn, Paul quickly shut off the mower. He could still hear the gardener's mower across the street. He had won the lawn mowing race. Paul laughed slyly and pushed his mower back to the front of his house so he could put it in the garage. He was dumbfounded by what he saw. The long-haired gardener had already finished the Henderson's backyard and was edging their driveway.

"No way!" Paul said in frustration as he shoved his mower into the garage. "That backyard is bigger than mine." Paul was almost going to accept defeat and cool off inside his house when a thought came over him. "This ain't over yet," he said with confidence as he eyed his overgrown shrubbery. "He may mow a lawn real fast, but it takes skill to trim a hedge."

Paul sharpened his hedge clippers and proceeded to give the gardener across the street a clinic in the art of hedge trimming. Paul's ego was further boosted when he saw the gardener retrieve a pair of hedge clippers from his van. Paul ignored him and concentrated even harder on his shrubbery. He could hear the gardener's shears busily snipping away at the Henderson's shrubs.

"Sounds like you're working too fast there, Mr. Gardener," Paul said in a quiet voice. "You take too much off a shrub and you'll screw the whole thing up."

Paul was nearly finished with his famous box pattern design when he heard Mrs. Henderson offer the gardener a cold drink. Paul admired his work. Each side of his shrubs was perfectly smooth and straight. He laughed to himself and then casually glanced over at the Henderson's shrubs.

"Ah, you've got to be *kidding!*" Paul said under his breath.

He threw the clippers on the ground and started for his front door. He glanced back again to see Mrs. Henderson admiring the way the gardener had transformed her ordinary shrubs into elaborate shapes and even animals.

Paul slammed the door as he walked into the living room. His daughter Rachel and her best friend Stacy sat in front of the T.V. Paul looked at them with irritation because of the pleasure they were experiencing in their relaxation.

"I'm out there struggling to get an even rectangle and Edward Scissorhands over across the street has no problem making sculptures out of *bushes.*"

"What're talking about, Dad?" Rachel asked. "We didn't do anything."

"No, not you two. I mean that idiot gardener over at the Henderson's. He just beat me at mowing the lawn and now he's over there like he's some kind of Michelangelo gardener or something. Stupid punk."

Rachel and Stacy jumped up and went to the window to marvel at the Henderson's new living statues.

"I'm sick of mowing that stupid yard. I hated doing it when I was a boy and I hate it even more now."

"Well, why don't you just hire someone to do the work for you?" Stacy asked.

Paul walked over to the window and looked out across the street. Mrs. Henderson was in the act of paying the miracle gardener.

"Yeah, maybe it's time to hire a lawn guy after all."

Paul was late for work again Monday morning. Rachel had already left for college. As Paul jogged out the door to get the morning paper he instantly noticed the same scruffy gardener parked in front of the Henderson's house. This time he was unloading lumber from the back of his dilapidated van.

"Now what the heck is the wonderman up to?" Paul asked himself.

Paul was too preoccupied with being late for work to give it another thought until he drove home late that afternoon. Sure enough, the gardener's van was still parked across the street. Paul did not see him anywhere so he went inside his house. As usual, Rachel and her friend Stacy were camped out in front of the T.V.

"Why don't you have your yard landscaped like the people across the street, Mr. B?" Stacy asked.

"Yeah Dad. I'm really embarrassed because our yard is so boring," Rachel added.

Paul was still irritated over the whole gardening thing and had no more patience for the subject.

"Why don't you two just watch your T.V. show? I didn't see either one of you out there in the heat helping me mow the lawn. I started mowing my father's lawn when I was in..."

"Second grade," Rachel and Stacy said in unison. "We know, Dad. You've told us about your childhood chores about a million times."

Paul looked at the girls in mock disgust.

"Oh, you kids would probably have a heat stroke if you had to do some of the work I did when I was a boy."

Later that afternoon as Paul was preparing dinner he looked out the kitchen window and saw Mrs. Henderson paying the gardener. Paul stepped closer to the kitchen window. Mrs. Henderson was obviously happy about whatever work the man had done for her. She smiled widely and kept patting him on the back as she walked him to his van.

Paul's curiosity about the gardener's lumber project was stirred even more. He knew that Mrs. Henderson walked with her friends in the evening so he decided to pretend to go jogging so he could accidentally run into her.

Later that evening Paul put on his athletic shoes and waited down a side street for Mrs. Henderson and her group of friends to come back from their walk. When Paul caught up to them Mrs. Henderson was just saying goodbye to her friends.

"How ya doin', Sarah?" Paul asked as he jogged up to her.

"Oh, hi Paul. I didn't know you jogged. I'm doing great. Life is good."

They started walking down the street together.

"Yeah, that's good. Say, I see your new lawn man was over at your house again. I saw him unloading some lumber this morning. Did he put in a few landscape timbers or something?"

Mrs. Henderson's face lit up.

"Isn't that man a genius? Did you see what he did with our shrubs?

Paul gave a tight smile and nodded. He almost bit his tongue. "So what did he do with the lumber?"

"Oh, the lumber?" Mrs. Henderson giggled. "He put in a deck for us."

Paul laughed sarcastically. "You mean he put in a landing area for you to step on from your patio door?"

"Oh no, I mean he built an entire deck."

Paul shook his head in disbelief. "He may mow a yard real fast, but I don't think a gardener can build an entire deck in a day."

Mrs. Harrison laughed at Paul's skepticism.

"Come on to my house and I'll show you."

Mrs. Harrison led Paul through her house to the sliding glass door that opened to her backyard. It was dark so Paul really could not see too well into the yard. Mrs. Harrison slid open the patio door and flicked on the flood lights.

"Good God almighty," Paul said aloud as he viewed the completed deck.

"I see you're as impressed as I was."

Paul walked over the decking and examined it closely. Every board was laid out perfectly and none of the decking seemed off level.

"Are you sure he had no help?"

"Well, I came out here and told him what I wanted and held a few boards for him so he could nail them, but he did all the work."

Paul continued to look over the deck. He was jealous of the man for his carpentry skills. Paul had always wanted to take care of all the carpentry and mechanical aspects around the house, but he was never any good at it.

By Friday Paul had pretty much forgotten about the gardener. He arrived home from work a bit early. As soon as Paul entered his house he could hear Rachel having a conversation with someone in the living room. Paul was taken aback by what he saw. There on the sofa with Rachel and her friend Stacy was the scruffy gardener.

"Oh, hi Daddy," Rachel said excitedly. "Look who knocked on the door looking for work. It's Jack."

Paul and the gardener both nodded to each other. Now that he had a close look at the gardener, Paul was amazed at how unkempt the man was. His clothes were filthy and his hair looked like it had not been washed in a couple of weeks. Paul suspected he was close to his age, but it was hard for him to tell.

Rachel and Stacy proceeded to beg Paul to hire Jack.

"Jack is a homeless vet. He can fix things and do all sorts of odd jobs," Rachel pleaded.

"Yeah, and remember what you said the other day about hating yard work, Mr. B.?" Stacy added.

Stacy and Rachel both started to hug Paul and pull at his arms.

"Oh, all right." Paul pulled away from the girls. "Uh, I guess the lawn could use some mowing and edging."

"I could straighten up those hedges for you," Jack said to the girls.

"Just the *lawn*," Paul said, irritated at having his hedgework criticized. "So where's that van of yours? Having engine trouble or something?"

"Nah, I'm parked over on the next street," Jack said as he stood to his feet. "I just cut through your backyard to save a trip to the front door."

<><><><>

Jack showed up late the next morning. He had hand-painted "Handy Man" on the driver's door of his van. Paul had already made up his mind to keep a close eye on him. He distrusted Jack mainly because of his appearance, but there was something else about him that made him suspicious.

Paul watched a little television, but frequently got up to look out the window. He was confounded even more because Jack was taking his time mowing the lawn.

"Oh, that's nice," Paul said to himself as he peered through the curtains at Jack. "Last week he was out there mowing as fast as The Flash with the Henderson's lawn. Now he's like a tortoise."

Just then he noticed Rachel and Stacy walking out on the lawn. They were giggling and nudging each other. Jack turned off the mower and talked to them for a few seconds before following the girls back into the house. Paul quickly moved away from the window and returned to his recliner.

Rachel and Stacy were still giggling when they entered the living room. Each of them had a hold of one of Jack's arms. They guided him over to the sofa and sat down on either side of him. The thought of a sweaty stranger sitting on the sofa with his daughter made Paul cringe.

Rachel and Stacy each bombarded Jack with questions.

"Why in the world are they talking this man's head off when he's supposed to be outside working?" Paul asked silently.

Rachel got up to go get Jack a cold drink, and immediately, Stacy jumped up in protest and the two raced each other to the kitchen. Stacy and Rachel argued over what drink to make Jack and who should bring it to him. Evidently, they compromised as one brought a glass and the other had Paul's last wine cooler.

After a good half hour Paul finally suggested to the girls that Jack really needed to go finish the lawn. Paul was met with evil stares from the girls, but Jack slowly rose and started out the door.

"Ah, this is an easy job, ladies." Jack glanced over at Paul. "I'll be available before you know it."

Rachel and Stacy hung around the windows constantly. The two wondered out loud if Jack needed another cold drink.

Paul could not believe the girls' fascination.

"What are you two fawning over such a thing as a lawn man?" Paul asked. "I wonder how old that guy is anyway? Besides, he looks like a creep."

"He is *not*," the two said in unison.

"A lot of men have long hair," Rachel interjected. "Maybe you're a little jealous because you're losing your hair, Dad."

"*Alright*, that's enough. We don't have to have a lawn man you know."

Jack finally finished mowing and edging the lawn. As a final insult, Jack went ahead and clipped the shrubs even though Paul had told him to leave them alone.

Paul grabbed his checkbook and Rachel and Stacy followed him out to the street. Jack was putting away his mower in the van when they approached.

"Uh, who do I make the check out to? I don't know your last name."

Jack crawled out of the back of his van.

"Oh, I really like to get paid in cash. It's better for me that way."

Paul sighed heavily.

"Rachel, could you go get my wallet?"

Rachel and Stacy were both gazing at the sweat-soaked Jack.

"*Rachel?* My wallet?"

She gave Paul an irritated look and then ran into the house.

Fortunately, Paul had just enough cash to pay Jack.

"Looks like them shutters and the trim under the eaves of your house needs repaintin'," Jack said as he stuffed the money into his shirt sleeve pocket.

Paul glanced around at his house and smirked.

"Well, I don't think I need to paint them. I'm gonna have that vinyl stuff put on instead."

"Oh, I've done lots of siding jobs. I can get all the materials and start on it Monday."

Rachel and Stacy were overjoyed.

"Please let him do the job, Dad," Rachel begged.

"Yeah, Mr. Benton, remember how good Jack was at putting in that deck for those people across the street?" Stacy pleaded.

Again, Rachel and Stacy both tugged at Paul's arms until he finally gave in.

"Would you let go of me? You two are acting like a couple of little girls." Paul turned to Jack. "I guess you can do that job for me. I just want it in white."

Jack smiled and looked at Rachel and Stacy. "Don't worry; I always aim to please."

<><><><>

Jack arrived early Monday morning. Rachel was still in her sleepwear when she opened the door and invited Jack inside. Paul tried to stop her, but he was too late. Paul repeatedly reminded Rachel to hurry up and get ready for her classes, but she ignored him and continued to talk with the obviously aroused Jack.

Just then Paul's coworker, Rob, drove up to give Paul a ride to the investment firm they worked for. Paul quickly invited his thirty year old coworker inside to break up the tension. Rachel finally went to get dressed and Paul was able to feel secure by locking Jack out of his house.

Rachel came back in the room and announced that her car was almost out of gas so Rob offered to take her to college.

Paul noticed Rob give Jack a strange look as they walked out to his car.

"So, would that carpenter guy be considered a hippie?" Rob asked Paul. "I'm way too young to remember those people."

"*Hey*, Jack's *not* a hippie," Rachel interrupted as she climbed in the back seat of Rob's car. "He just happens to have long hair."

Rob shrugged his shoulders.

"Ok, ok, don't bite my head off. But, what's up with the military jacket in the middle of the summer? Is he a Vietnam vet or something?"

"Nah, he's no where near old enough to have gone to Vietnam," Paul answered. "I guess that *he* thinks he's from that whole 60's era though."

Later, Paul and Rob's coworkers had lunch at their favorite restaurant. Soon the subject turned to cars and car repair woes. Rob explained that his parents were having trouble with their car. The office manager, who lives two streets over from Paul, suggested that Rob take his car to a mechanic named Jack.

"Well, what garage does this Jack guy work at?" Rob asked as he spooned some more pico de gallo sauce on his fajitas.

"Oh, he doesn't have a garage. He just goes around the neighborhood doing odd jobs."

Immediately, Paul and Rob looked at each other.

"Does he have long hair and was he wearing a military jacket?" Paul asked, already knowing the answer.

"Yeah, that's *him*." the office manager said through a mouthful of tortilla chips. "So, you know him, huh?"

Paul smirked and nodded.

"Yeah, that guy can fix anything," the manager continued. "I took my Beemer to the dealership five or six times and they couldn't fix it. That Jack guy fixed it in about thirty minutes." Again, he plunged another tortilla chip into the bowl of salsa. "He sure saved my car. I was gonna sell it before that."

Paul was pleasantly surprised to see new vinyl fascia trim and shutters on his house as he pulled into his driveway. Although Jack's van was still parked outside, Paul couldn't find him until he walked into his living room. Jack was once again sitting on the sofa between the giggling Rachel and Stacy.

"Oh, there you are. So, you finished the whole house, huh?"

Jack quickly looked at Rachel and then Stacy.

"Nah, the back of the house and one side is the same."

"You mean you couldn't finish the job when you did a whole deck in a day for the Henderson's across the street?" Paul asked condescendingly.

"Dad, *I* told Jack to stop working so he could come inside the house and cool off," Rachel said with frustration.

Paul frowned at his daughter upon hearing the revelation.

"So are you wantin' me to put a deck in your backyard?" Jack asked. "It could use some sprucin' up."

"*Yeah*," Rachel and Stacy said in unison.

"*No*," Paul said bluntly as he looked directly at Jack.

Paul sat down in his recliner and began opening his newspaper.

Rachel made a face and then proceeded to flirt with Jack. Paul became even angrier when this time Jack began making eyes back at his little girl.

"O.K., I think it's time to call it a day," Paul said as he quickly rose to his feet. "Jack can finish up tomorrow."

"*Dad!* Stacy and I planned on making supper for Jack," Rachel complained.

"Well, that's nice, but he has to leave now."

Rachel hardly spoke to her father the rest of the evening.

That night Paul could not stop thinking of Jack and his daughter. When he finally fell asleep he had a dream. In the dream it was five years in the future and he was evidently at Rachel's wedding. Paul proudly escorts her down the aisle and is shocked when the groom turns around and it is Jack. He is still wearing his military jacket.

Paul was awakened the next day by someone honking their car horn. As he made his way down the hall, Rachel rushed past him.

"Bye! My ride is here!" Rachel screamed as she ran to the door.

Paul looked out the window and saw Rachel about to climb into Jack's van. Immediately, he ran outside not caring that he was dressed only in his pajama bottoms.

"Rachel, *I'll* give you a ride," Paul said as he ran up to the van.

Rachel quickly slammed the door shut and rolled down the window.

"But Dad, you'll just embarrass me dressed like that." Rachel nodded for Jack to leave and they backed out of the driveway.

"Well that does it right there," Paul said aloud as he watched Jack's van speed away. "I'll let him finish the house, but I'll never hire him to do anything else. I can't believe it, but it looks like my little girl might think she's in love with the creep."

Paul became worried after it had been plenty of time for Jack to have gotten back from dropping off Rachel at college. He got dressed quickly and decided to drive by the college. He spotted Jack's van near the business building's parking lot. Rachel was leaning on the driver's side window talking to Jack. Rachel did not even notice when Paul pulled up beside them.

"Rachel! You get to class!" Rachel turned and frowned at her father. "Girl, you've never been late to a class in your life." Rachel slowly turned and started walking towards the business building. Paul was about to tell Jack to get to work on his house, but he just stared at him. There was a hypnotic quality in Jack's eyes that Paul had never noticed. After a few moments Paul realized he was late and took off for work.

Paul was pleasantly surprised to find his house finished when he came home from work. However, Jack was not there and neither was Rachel. The tension and anger built up in Paul as the evening progressed. Finally, at about nine that night, Jack and Rachel entered the house laughing. Without delay, Paul took out his checkbook and pen.

"O.K, how much do I owe you for the work?"

Jack glanced down at the check book in Paul's hands and smiled.

"Ah, it's like I said; I only take cash."

Paul sighed heavily.

"Fine. We can do that. Rachel and I will go to the ATM machine then."

"Oh, I can get the money for Jack."

"No. Jack will wait outside for us."

On the way to the ATM, Paul let Rachel know about his thoughts on the situation.

"Look, I've got no more work for Jack. I don't want you seeing that man anymore."

Rachel said nothing. Tears started streaming down her face.

As Paul headed back to his house he could not wait to confront Jack. All day long he had planned out exactly what he was going to say. Rachel was on Paul's heels as he walked out to the street. Jack was leaning against his van smoking a cigarette.

"Uh, I have no more work for you," Paul said uneasily as he handed Jack the money.

Jack smiled at Rachel and then looked Paul in the eye.

"Are you sure about that, Paul?"

He had that same hypnotic look in his eyes Paul had noticed earlier at the college. Dracula eyes. Just then an automatic sprinkler kicked on down the street. It was just enough of a distraction to jar Paul back to his senses. A moment longer and Paul might have backed down.

"Uh, yeah. No more work."

Jack smiled again and gazed at Rachel before climbing into his van. He drove off slowly and paused a full minute at the stop sign just down the street. Paul could see him watching them in his side mirror.

Paul kicked himself for not saying the things he had practiced in his mind. It was Jack's hypnotic eyes again that had stopped him. He tried to put his hand on Rachel's shoulder to walk with her back inside the house, but she flinched.

"Hate you," Rachel said as she ran into the house and slammed the door.

Fortunately, Paul never saw Jack around the neighborhood the next week. He tried to resume his relationship with Rachel, but she remained aloof.

After a few days though, Rachel was suddenly happy again. She began going out at night saying that she would be with friends or with Stacy. Paul suspected that she might be going out with Jack, but he did not want to risk following her.

Much to Paul's frustration, Jack got a job house-sitting at the house next to the Henderson's across the street. Paul began noticing Stacy's car parked across the street more and more frequently. It would not be long before Rachel would be visiting Jack; if she had not started already. Paul knew it was time for action.

Paul bought Rob's lunch the next day at work. It did not take Rob long to realize that Paul wanted something.

"Alright man, what do you want? Rob asked bluntly. "Do you have a high maintenance client that you want to push off on me or something?"

"I need your help with Rachel," Paul stated seriously. "I think she's still seeing that handy man."

Rob cringed as he put down his fork. He now gave his full attention to Paul.

"Yeah, I'm talking about that long-haired handy man who lives in his van." Paul sighed for a moment. "I'm desperate. You don't know what it's like with my daughter. Rachel is all I've got, man, since my wife died. I can't say no to Rachel easily."

"So what do you want me to do? Just name it, man."

"I want you to get your brother Steve to go out with Rachel."

"*Get* him to go out with her? OK, Rachel and all her friends were crazy about Steve when he was in high school and you wouldn't let him around Rachel because you said he was too much of a stud. Are you forgetting that?"

"I know, I know," Paul groaned. "This is an emergency situation and I'm desperate." Paul leaned in close to Rob.

"Look, just have him start taking Rachel out and I mean *regularly*, man."

Paul enlisted Stacy's help to set things up with Steve. After some convincing, Rachel finally agreed to go out with Steve. Steve was a couple of years older than Rachel and was a senior at the university. He was the kind of young man who had it all. He was athletic, looked like a model, and was regularly on the dean's list.

Paul was pleasantly surprised to see Steve drive up in his new sports car. He was absolutely overjoyed when he noticed Jack peering from behind the curtains across the street as Rachel slipped into Steve's car.

"Oh, this must be my lucky day," Paul commented to himself as he watched Steve's car drive away. "Just don't touch my daughter."

Paul worried about Rachel all evening. His biggest concern was that she would actually prefer Jack to Steve.

Rachel came back home just past midnight. Paul jumped to his feet and met Rachel at the door.

"Well?" Paul took a quick look across the street to see if Jack was watching as

Steve's car sped away. "How did it go? Did you like Steve? Was he good to you?"

"Dad! One question at a time." Rachel plopped down on the sofa. After a couple of tense seconds she smiled. "It was nice. It was *real* nice."

Paul sat down next to her.

"Yeah? Nice, huh? Will you see him again because I gotta tell you I like the guy."

"Yes, Dad," Rachel said as she rolled her eyes. "We're going out again tomorrow."

Rachel smiled and hugged him. It had seemed like such a long time since they had hugged. Paul had a hard time getting to sleep because he was excited that his plan was working.

Steve and Rachel continued to date throughout the week. Paul had not been so happy in months. His plan was working beautifully. Paul took every opportunity to gloat at Jack across the street as he sat on the front porch and watched Steve pick up Rachel for their dates.

On Friday night Paul noticed that Rachel was still at home. He sat down next to her on the sofa.

"Hey, what're you doing here watching T.V.? Is Steve late to pick you up or something?"

"Oh, he's not late or anything," Rachel said as she continued to stare at the television set.

"Well, what's the deal then, daughter?" Paul asked, halfway irritated.

"Steve's kind of, well, icky."

"*Icky?* Paul said in disgust. "That smart, clean cut boy with the nice clothes and beautiful car is *icky?*"

"Well, yeah, Dad."

"How in the world can you think that?" Paul got up and began to pace. "Now, that handy man, Jack, *he* was icky with his filthy hair and clothes that were..."

Paul stopped when he noticed tears running down Rachel's face.

"I know that you set me up with Steve to get me away from Jack," Rachel sobbed. "The truth is that I'm happier with Jack. Going out with Steve has helped me see just how much I love Jack."

Paul's heart sank. He stared a moment at Rachel and then slowly walked to his bedroom and shut the door. Just fifteen minutes ago he had felt ten feet tall and now the situation seemed almost hopeless. Paul picked up the phone and called Rob to tell him the plan had failed.

Paul spent most of the night trying to sleep, but his mind was too preoccupied with Jack and Rachel. Paul wished that he could get Rachel to see Jack as he saw him. Paul had no doubt that Jack was hiding some things about his life that just might make Rachel turn away from him. Paul decided to find out more about Jack so that Rachel would forget him.

Paul waited a day before implementing his new strategy. He suggested to Rachel that maybe he and Jack should get to know one another. Paul would learn all he could about the man while diffusing Rachel's excitement over dating a man that her father forbade her to see. Rachel had been planning a swimming party at the house where Jack had been staying. Rachel reluctantly agreed to let her father come to the party. Paul invited Rob to go along with him. Their plan was for Paul to keep Jack busy while Rob went through Jack's belongings.

When they arrived at the party Rob and Paul were a bit surprised to see Jack without his trademark military jacket. It took every bit of strength that he had, but Paul managed to strike up a meaningless conversation with Jack. After a couple of minutes Jack removed his shirt. He had approximately ten tattoos of the prison variety on his chest and back. Rob and Paul looked at each other for a moment to gauge one another's reaction to the tattoos. Paul noticed a small, circular scar on Jack's shoulder.

"I guess that's a cigar burn, huh?" Paul asked Jack, figuring the wound was self-inflicted.

"Nah, that ain't no cigar burn. It's just a bullet hole," Jack said bluntly.

"Well, uh, that's cool, I guess," Rob said as he stared hypnotically at the scar for a moment. He then broke out of his miniature trance. "I'm gonna go to the little boys' room," he said as he patted Paul on the shoulder. "Don't worry Mr. Jack, I'll find it by myself."

Paul gave Rob a quick nod of approval. It was now his duty to keep Jack occupied while Rob went through his things inside the house.

Paul had planned on trying to get Jack to reveal some things about himself and his past. It did not take two minutes for Jack's hypnotic persona to take its effect on Paul. Rather than finding out about Jack, Paul wound up talking about his own life. In any event, the one-sided conversation did allow Rob sufficient time to go through Jack's belongings.

Paul was greatly relieved when he saw Rob coming down the hallway that led to the bedrooms. Rob stared straight ahead as he exited the sliding glass door and walked briskly towards Paul and Jack.

"Let's go, man," Rob said without a hint of emotion.

Paul desperately wanted to stay at the party to keep an eye on Rachel, but Rob's speedy exit had him fascinated to hear if he had discovered something back in the bedroom. Paul was just about to walk over to tell Rachel that he was leaving when Jack lifted her off her feet and threw her into the pool. He then did a belly flop next to her. Rachel and Jack were so busy laughing and splashing around that neither one heard Paul say good-bye.

Rob was already waiting for Paul on his front porch. He was still in an anxious mood.

"Man, what took you so long to get over here?"

Paul shrugged.

"Just trying to say good-bye to my daughter. You act like you found something."

Rob motioned for Paul to unlock his front door so they could talk privately. Paul took a seat in his recliner. Rob stood near him and fidgeted.

"Well, what did you see?"

"Huh?" Rob said as he was clearly in deep thought. "Oh, yeah. Do you know how much clothes that guy has? We're talking two shirts and two pair of filthy underwear!"

"That's it? That's *all* you found out? You dragged me away from the party to tell me that?"

"Oh, no." Rob smiled. "I found the guy's wallet. I'm telling you, there must have been at least $2000 in there. At least."

Paul raised his eyebrows.

"There's more, Paul. I also saw his driver's license. It was from Alaska. It's been expired for a few years. Get a load of this, man. His last name is Shumaker and he's freakin' older than you by *three* months. Oh yeah, I also saw a loaded handgun."

Paul shook his head. "Well, the fickle finger of fate has done poked me in the eye."

Paul hardly slept at all that night. His mind was in a daze for several hours before he could think straight enough to decide on another plan of action.

On Monday Paul and Rob took off work an hour early to meet with an investigator who had helped Rob's aunt. Although he was terribly expensive, he promised to have some useful information by the end of the week. The investigator pointed out that Jack was not violating any laws since Rachel was an adult. Paul was still hopeful. He felt like this was just about his last chance.

Fortunately, Rachel was home when Paul arrived from his visit with the investigator. She seemed in a good mood so Paul made small talk with her before discussing Jack.

"Rach, don't you know the man is the same age as *me*? Think about that. *Really* think about that. He's the same age as your old man here. You're only twenty. You've got to end this."

Rachel shook her head.

"I love him, Dad. I'll run away with him if I have to."

Paul decided to back off for a few days until the investigation of Jack was completed. In the meantime, Rachel and Stacy had a falling out over Jack. Rachel suspected Stacy was jealous of their relationship.

Paul steered clear of the subject of Jack with Rachel, but he tried to keep a sharp eye on the house across the street. Paul learned from Mrs. Henderson that her neighbors would be returning in the next few days. Mrs. Henderson had spoken with Jack about it and he hinted that he would be hitting the road soon. Paul was also disturbed to find several wedding magazines in Rachel's room. She had circled a couple of odd looking dresses. There was even a magazine for biker weddings.

One evening Paul was especially excited when he noticed the investigator's number come up on the caller ID.

"Did you find something out?" Paul asked without even saying hello.

"Uh, Mr. Benton, we're following some leads," the investigator stated. "Seems like there's not many states this Shumaker hasn't lived in. Mr. Benton, if you really want our team to pursue this case to the fullest, I'm going to have some travel expenses. I need to fly to Alaska and a couple other states. I'll need an additional payment."

"You want *more* money?"

"Mr. Benton, you have to realize a proper investigation rarely centers on one person. We've got to investigate the people that Shumaker has been involved with."

"Alright, but get back here ASAP because it's looking like Jack will be hitting the road in a few days."

"You'll still have our full report by the end of the week as promised."

That Friday, as Paul was leaving for work he noticed that Stacy's luggage was missing from the hall closet.

"Oh Lord," Paul said as he slammed the closet door shut. "You better have something for me today, Mr. Investigator.

Paul had a difficult time concentrating at work. He kept checking the time. He had also called the investigator's office three times before noon. Each time Paul was told the investigator had not yet returned from out of state.

Paul was about to leave his office when the receptionist buzzed him that he had a phone call. It was the investigator.

"Mr. Benton? I apologize for not returning your messages from this morning. I just flew in from Alabama."

"Alabama? I thought you were in Alaska?" Paul asked.

"Yes sir, I was in Alaska earlier in the week. I've actually been to five states this week to follow up on some of Shumaker's, uh, shall we say, acquaintances. Mr.

Benton, when could I meet with you to go over the investigation? I think you will be..."

"I'll be right over," Paul interrupted.

Paul grabbed Rob out of his office and the two sped away to the investigator's office. Paul ran a stop sign and a traffic light along the way.

Paul was pleased to see the investigator talking with the receptionist when he entered the office.

"Oh, Mr. Benton? You sure got over here in a hurry," the investigator said as he motioned for him and Rob to come into his office.

The investigator pulled a large binder out of his luggage and plopped it down on the desk.

"I came here straight from the airport." The investigator tapped the large binder. "As you can see we were able to pull quite a bit of information about Shumaker. I've got to admit he's been a particularly hard nut to crack. If I hadn't of done some personal interviews I think this binder would be rather thin."

"OK, I've got it," Paul said. His anxiety was at the breaking point. "I'm not surprised this was a hard case. Now, what do you have that will help me convince my daughter not to marry this guy because it's looking like that's where it's headed."

The investigator put on his reading glasses and leafed through the binder.

"As I said on the phone, this Shumaker has lived in a number of states. I can tell you right now that he was never in the military."

"I knew it," Rob said as he elbowed Paul.

The investigator continued.

"And there is an arrest record for assault, disorderly conduct, D.U.I, and possession of a controlled substance."

Paul shifted in his chair and sighed heavily.

"Mr. Benton, are you alright?"

Paul nodded.

"You said you need some evidence to help convince your daughter not to marry this man. I'd like to show you a video interview I conducted yesterday afternoon in Alabama."

Both Paul and Rob moved to the edge of their seats. Beads of sweat started to form on Paul's forehead.

"I realize you paid quite a bit of money for our travel expenses. We've actually saved you some money by doing the interviews through the video rather than flying them here to the office." The investigator removed a video camera from his luggage. "I'll have to show you the interview on the camera screen. I'll have someone make you a copy before you leave today." The investigator fast forwarded through several video clips before finding the one he wanted to show. "Ah, here we are, Huntsville, Alabama." The investigator said as he turned the camera around so Paul and Rob could see the screen.

The video showed a woman who was obviously living in a low-income apartment. There were several noisy children in the background so it was difficult to hear the conversation. The investigator handed the lady a photo of Jack Shumaker and asked her if she knew the man in the photo.

"Yep, that's him alright," the lady said as a small boy with a filthy shirt climbed onto her lap. "Here's your daddy," she said as she handed the photo to the boy.

The investigator continued his questioning of the lady. "Now, ma'am, just how acquainted are you with Jack Shumaker?"

"*Acquainted?* Well, just how acquainted does a person have to be if they're *married?*"

Paul leaned back in his chair and smiled at the ceiling. Rob patted him on the back. The lady continued.

"He skipped out and left me to deal with all this. Two of these kids are his." She looked into the camera. "Jack, you better get your butt back here and face reality, mister!"

"So, he's married and has kids?" Paul asked.

"Actually, this is his second wife. Shumaker never divorced her, and he illegally married another woman in Nevada. She's nineteen."

"Nailed him to the wall!" Rob said loudly. "I told you this guy is the best, Paul."

Paul glanced at his watch. "Look, I need to get to my daughter. Can I just take this camera and show her? We can't wait for a copy."

The investigator handed the camera to Paul and he and Rob ran out the door. Paul again ran several stop signs as he raced to get home to show Rachel what they found out about Jack.

"God, I just hope we're not too late," Paul said as he screeched the car to a halt in front of his garage door.

Paul ran into the house and began shouting for Rachel. He started to panic when he noticed that Rachel was not in the house and her luggage was gone as well.

"She's not here!" Paul said as he grabbed Rob.

"Let's go check and see if she's with Jack across the street," Rob said as he turned to run out the front door.

As they neared the driveway to the house they both realized that Jack's van was no longer there. Paul tried the front door, but it was locked. He was in a full panic now.

"*Rachel!*" he screamed. "Oh, God, I've lost my little girl."

Rob grabbed Paul. "Come on man, let's check the back door!"

When they got around to the back of the house they noticed that the back door was slightly opened. Paul ran through the house again screaming for Rachel. They eventually found her in a hallway. She was slumped against the wall and seemed to be in a trance. Her luggage was next to her.

"I came here to tell Jack to run away with me so we could get married," Rachel sobbed. "It's over, Daddy". She noticed Rob standing there. Rachel straightened up a bit and wiped her eyes with her shirt. "I found Jack- with *Stacy*!"

Paul helped Rachel to her feet and held her for awhile. "Come on, girl, let's go home." Paul handed Rachel's luggage to Rob. "I better call Stacy's parents when we get back to our house."

"Why, Daddy?"

"Because we just found out that Jack is still married, sweetheart."

Rachel buried her head in Paul's chest and began crying again. Paul stayed with Rachel back inside their house until she was relaxed enough to rest. He realized that Rob was still waiting for him on the driveway.

"I don't want to ever go through something like this again," Paul said as he patted Rob on the back.

"Well, how's she doing?" Rob said as nodded towards the house.

"That girl is absolutely crushed. It's gonna take some time for her to get over this one."

Paul motioned for Rob to get into the car so he could drive him back to his car at their workplace.

"I tell you what; I wouldn't have made it through all this without your help."

Rob smiled. "I guess we should have used Stacy instead of my brother."

Paul laughed. "Yeah, I guess so." Paul started the car, but paused before backing out the driveway. "Rob, I owe you big time, man. I'm gonna give you my covered parking space at work. I'll trade you my best two clients for your two worst. Just name it and I'll do it."

Rob thought for a moment and then looked at Paul's house for a second. "Well, I guess there is one thing."

"Name it, buddy."

"Can I take out Rachel sometime?"

# CASE OF FATE

John Denton paused at the heavily lacquered office door and read the sign next to it. *Lawrence Kucinski, M.D. Psychiatry.* John cautiously entered the waiting area and walked up to the receptionist's desk.

"Could you tell Dr. Kucinski that John Denton is here?"

The receptionist glanced at the appointment book on her desk. "Yes sir. I'll let the doctor know right now. Please have a seat, Mr. Denton."

The receptionist knocked softly on the door behind her desk and disappeared for a moment.

John took a seat on the leather sofa behind a coffee table. He shifted position on the sofa several times and drummed on his thighs. He scanned the walls of the waiting area. There were many photos of Dr. Kucinski posing with police chiefs, politicians and ordinary police officers. Above the sofa hung a huge frame of at least twenty police department patches from all over the country. Near the door to Kucinski's office were photos of him with a couple of famous talk show hosts and pop psychologists. John reached into his jeans pocket and removed a small digital audio recorder. "Just in case this guy wants to hypnotize me and make me say something I'll regret later," he thought to himself. John could hear that the receptionist was nearing the doorway to the waiting area so he quickly pressed the record button and pocketed the recorder.

The receptionist returned and announced that Dr. Kucinski could see him now.

Dr. Kucinski's office had bookshelves on every wall. John was surprised to see he had a wide variety of fiction books as well as many books from his field of psychiatry. The paintings on the walls were traditional landscapes, but with a peculiar twist. One landscape of a deer drinking from a stream had a small child in a tree above the deer. The child looked almost as if he were ready to pounce on the deer. John realized a scene of a mountain in another painting was really an illusion of a person smiling. A twenty gallon aquarium was on a stand in the corner, but had no fish inside it. Dr. Kucinski only displayed his bachelor's degree- in chemistry. John thought it strange that he would not have his master's degree, and especially his medical degree, displayed as well. There were two large leather recliners near the window with a small round table between them and another doorway that John assumed was a restroom or closet. There were several family photos behind Kucinski's desk. John figured one was of Mrs. Kucinski and the other Kucinski's daughter with her children.

Dr. Kucinski was seated at his desk. He was obviously having some difficulty using a tablet computer.

"I sure do miss the feel of a real keyboard. I don't think I'll every get used to these touch screens." He came around his desk and extended his hand. "Mr. Denton? It's pleasure to meet you. I'm Lawrence Kucinski."

Dr. Kucinski was short and had thinning hair. John estimated he was in his early sixties. Dr. Kucinski had extremely pale blue eyes. In fact, they were the lightest color of blue John had ever seen.

John took a seat in front of the desk and Dr. Kucinski returned to his office chair. "So, Mr. Denton, what brings you here today?"

"First off, I gotta say this is one of the last places I thought I would ever be."

Dr. Kucinski laughed loudly. "I believe I've heard that one before. Just know you're welcome. I'm here to help you in any way I can."

"Well, I've got an old coworker, Moses Becker?"

Dr. Kucinski nodded and smiled. "Yes, I remember him well. So I take it you are in law enforcement? How is Sergeant Becker?"

"He's doing real good now. Yeah, I was a detective, but I'm retired now. Moe Becker thought you could help me. He was pretty messed up when he had to shoot that teenager who pulled a gun on him. I didn't think he'd ever get over that, but he said you had a lot to do with it."

"Well, Detective Denton, I wouldn't credit myself entirely for Mr. Becker's recovery. I get quite a few referrals from police departments to help out officers who are on administrative leave for discharging their weapon in the line of duty."

"That's one of the reasons I came to you. You probably understand us cops better than the average shrink would."

"You've already taken the biggest step, Detective Denton, by walking through my office door."

John managed a tight smile. "It's like I said, Doctor, I've never been to a mental doctor before. I'm just glad my insurance will pay for most of it." John laughed nervously. Dr. Kucinski nodded and smiled. "I know you helped out Moe, but I gotta tell you I'm not sure you'll be able to help me. Unless you know how to erase parts of people's memories." John motioned towards the waiting area doorway. "I saw that picture of you when you were on that guy's talk show. I can't say that I like the host, but I saw that episode." Dr. Kucinski again nodded and smiled. "You know, Doctor, you and me met one time? It was fifteen years ago at a violent crimes symposium in D.C. You did a workshop about the motivations of serial killers in one of the breakout sessions."

"I hope the session was beneficial to you, Detective. I'm still invited to do that workshop every year at the symposium. I've written several articles in professional journals and even wrote a couple of books on the topic."

"Yeah, I know. I read your books."

"Hopefully they weren't too dry for you Detective Denton," Kucinski said with a laugh.

"Nah, they were real helpful. I just had to keep a dictionary close by. You sure use a lot of fifty dollar words."

John and Dr. Kucinski shared a laugh. "Well, you probably wouldn't like the project I'm currently writing. It's a textbook for the FBI academy- lots of fifty words. I only see a couple of clients now in the morning and a couple in the afternoon. I find that I can get more work done on the textbook here in my office." Dr. Kucinski motioned to the photo of him with two young girls behind his desk. "We're keeping our granddaughters with us while my daughter and her husband are overseas. They're in the military. Let's just say my house can get rather, lively."

"Yeah, I can imagine. Well, the fact that you know about investigations, and my buddy Moe's advice, is what sold me on making an appointment. So here I am."

Dr. Kucinski stood and motioned for John to join him in the chairs near the window. "It's a bit too formal for me to talk with you across the desk. These chairs are just about as comfortable as you will ever find, Detective."

John settled in to one of the leather recliners. "Ah, yeah, I see what you mean, Doctor. I could use one of these chairs at my house. I hope I don't fall asleep on you."

Dr. Kucinski took a seat in the recliner beside John. "Well, I can't say that I haven't had a client fall asleep in one of these chairs. As a matter of fact it's happened on three occasions."

John took in the view from the twelfth floor window. "Wow, you can see quite a bit from here. I think I would move the desk by this window."

Dr. Kucinski chuckled. "I'm afraid I wouldn't get much work done if I did that. On a clear day you can see Alcatraz fairly well. Too bad it's cloudy out."

"Where's the couch? I thought all you guys had one with a chair next to it so you can sit and write stuff down."

"I'm afraid most of us in the profession don't operate in that manner, Detective Denton." Dr. Kucinski opened up a notebook and held it up. "We do still use these." He wrote down John's name and the date. "Let me start by getting some background information about you. Your family growing up, schools you attended, employment, those sorts of things."

John nodded. "Well, I grew up over in San Patricio which is about an hour from here. My father ran a forklift at the lumberyard and mother took care of my sister and me. I went to high school and then did four years in the Army. I finished college and became a cop back in San Patricio. I did that for six years and then I was promoted to detective. My interest was in homicide, but in that town if you were a detective you investigated every kind of crime. Course, we had a homicide about once every ten years, if that. So, I did that for about nineteen years and then another four years at a different department and then I retired." John looked over at Dr. Kucinski's notepad. "Is this all there is to it?"

"What exactly do you mean?" Dr. Kucinski asked as he set his pen on top of the notepad.

"I mean this therapy stuff. All we're gonna do is just kind of talk to each other?"

Dr. Kucinski nodded. "That's a good way of putting it. It's all about conversation essentially."

"Well, then I guess I can do this. I thought you were going to want to know all about my fantasies or something."

Again, Dr. Kucinski laughed. "I wouldn't compare what you've seen in movies and on television to what I do. Just think of me as sort of an advisor."

John nodded and smiled. "An advisor? I like that. Well, I'll be needing some advising."

Dr. Kucinski picked up his notebook and pen again. "Now, Detective Denton, we've become acquainted and I believe I have an adequate amount of background information about you." He checked off a couple of items on his notes. "Let's get to the nature of your visit today. You said earlier that you'd like to have certain memories erased. Now, I have had success with clients using hypnotherapy, but I can assure you it would not be effective in such cases. We really can not erase memories."

"Yeah, I guess I figured that much, Doctor."

"Detective, are you able to tell me about some of the memories you wish you could have erased?"

John shifted position in the recliner a couple of times and then cleared his throat.

"I can tell you." Now he stared out the window rather than looking at Dr. Kucinski. "All this started eighteen years ago. I was thirty-five then. That's when I was a detective in my hometown. There were only about five thousand people in San Patricio so our police force was small and we had a very limited budget. Course, the major crimes we had were domestic violence, drugs and burglary. Like I said, I was involved in the investigation of all types of crime. I had taken some training in homicide investigating, but we hadn't had a murder in over fifteen years. One day we got a call that somebody found the body of a young woman out by the lake. Being a small town, I was not only the homicide department, but the crime scene technician as well. The woman had been strangled. She was fresh out of nursing school and had taken a job at our clinic about six months earlier. So, as I learned from my training I looked at the people she knew. Not many people around knew her since she had just moved to town. All her relatives and friends she knew back in her home town came up clean. They were just as baffled as to why anyone would want to kill her. I went about my other duties and kept an ear open for any information. This went on for about a year and then I got a call about a lady who was found dead in her house. She was about sixty and lived alone. I had gone to high school with one of her nieces. It was spooky because it seemed to be one of those deaths of what they call an undetermined nature. That lady didn't have a bruise or a mark on her. There were no fluid samples on her to get and trace evidence was just not there. My chief figured she died of natural causes, but I wasn't so sure. I went ahead and treated it as a homicide investigation until I heard what the official cause of death was. The medical examiner did the autopsy and really didn't find anything. It wasn't until about two months later that we learned she had been poisoned. There was no trace of poison on any of the cups or plates in her kitchen. We even tested her toothbrush. It was a mystery as to how the poison got into her system. I had absolutely no leads whatsoever. I went as far back in her past as

I could go and interviewed no telling how many people, but I just drew a blank. Early on, I started to wonder if this and the other death were related. I started to do a lot research on ViCAP." John stopped and looked over at Dr. Kucinski. "Do you know what that is, Doctor?"

"I'm familiar with the violent crimes database, Detective."

"Oh, OK." John continued. "I spent a lot of time understanding the database so I could research and see if there were other cases that were similar. You see, I had a hunch that we had a serial killer. Well, I found out there were four cases in different states where someone had died of undetermined causes and it turned out to be poison. There was also one just over in San Francisco. I didn't have any DNA evidence, but I found out it may not have mattered because not all the DNA samples make it to the national registry. The trace evidence from my two cases was nothing special, but I wanted to know if the trace evidence from these similar cases would link up. Well, trace evidence is handled by different labs. Even though we were pretty close to each other, our department used a different lab than the San Francisco P.D."

John rose from his chair and leaned on the window sill. The sky cleared briefly and he could see Alcatraz Island. "My biggest obstacle of all was my chief. He tried to run the investigations and he wouldn't get me the resources I asked for. Our P.D. got no help from the state. My boss was not convinced at all that the two deaths were committed by the same person. He kept reminding me that only one per cent of murders are committed by a serial killer. I tried to get a criminal profiler to help us out, but the budget wouldn't allow it. Eventually I could see a pattern where someone would die of an undetermined cause and then just about a year later there would be another murder close to the same neighborhood."

John noticed he could no longer see the island. He returned to the recliner.

"We got a television news crew from San Francisco to come out and do a story in hopes it would spur some leads. I was furious with my chief for telling the reporter some important information about the murders. Of course this information was leaked out and it really hurt the case. We didn't get many good leads from the report and the case stayed cold. A couple of years later I found out from an acquaintance with the San Francisco P.D. that they had two suspicious deaths that were unsolved. After some digging I found out one of the victims had a similar poison in her system. I threw myself back into the investigation."

John rose again and started to pace around the office. "Is it alright if I walk around when I'm talking? I'm a little keyed up."

Dr. Kucinski set his pen down and looked up at John. "You do whatever is comfortable for you. There are no set of rules for this. Communication is the key. It doesn't matter how that takes place; just as long as it does."

John nodded and continued. "I spent a lot of time running down empty leads and all this put a strain on my family. I didn't say anything about my family to you earlier. Back then I had a wife and two kids. My wife said I was obsessed with the two women who were murdered. She told me that I should just let them rest in peace and quit giving their families false hope. My wife got on to me for not spending any time with my son and daughter. I didn't change and she separated from me and then filed for divorce a few months later."

John looked over at Dr. Kucinski to see how many notes he had written on his pad. He plopped back down in the recliner.

"My boss told me to lay off the cases, but I continued my investigation on my own time with my own money. He warned me to stop what I was doing and let him handle the cases, but I continued on. I talked with the prosecutor's office without permission. My chief retaliated against me by demoting me and giving me a desk job. He also made me take some time off. I traveled to the FBI headquarters to try and get their help, but I didn't get anywhere. This is when I went to D.C. and met you at that symposium. Well, the chief found out that I had contacted the FBI and he let me have it. He met with the city council and I was fired from the department. I had burned up just about all my savings. I didn't know what to do."

"This was quite a turning point in your life," Dr. Kucinski noted. "Where did you go from there?"

"Where did I *go*? I went to the nearest bar. I pretty much gave up on life and tried to drink my problems away." John managed a tight smile. "I ran into Moe Becker one day. We had worked together when we were officers with the department.

Moe was working in a small city not too far from here. He convinced his boss to hire me as a detective. Evidently, my new chief had spoken to my old boss because I was only allowed to work burglaries. But, I continued to research unsolved cases that were similar to the two killings. I wasn't going to give up."

"I'm sure the families appreciated your tenacity, Detective."

John looked down at his feet. "I hope they did. I know my family didn't. My kids didn't want much to do with me and I guess I don't blame them."

John looked out the window again to see if the clouds had cleared. He sighed loudly. "So, I worked that burglary job for a few years and then I almost had a heart attack at fifty-one. It happened right there at my desk. I had triple bypass surgery the next morning. My doctor said I was lucky. I went ahead and retired a couple of months after that."

John looked up and shook his head. "It always bothered me that I never could quite figure the guy out- the killer I mean. It was obvious that he was intelligent and probably was a person nobody would suspect. I could tell he traveled quite a bit. The motivation was the hardest part. He didn't seem to have any one kind of victim in mind, except that they either lived alone or were alone when they were killed. The best I could come up with was that he was most likely some kind of predator."

They were interrupted by a buzzing tone from Dr. Kucinski's phone. It was the receptionist letting him know it was almost 5:30 and that she would be leaving for the day. Dr. Kucinski went to the door to tell the receptionist good bye.

"Well, Detective Denton, I believe we have had a most productive conversation."

"You mean that's it for the day? John asked. "I was hoping you could tell me how to get all this out of my mind. I can't tell you how many nightmares I've had."

Dr. Kucinski shut the door to the waiting area and smiled. "Oh, absolutely. We can continue. You've been talking for almost two hours. I apologize for not offering you a beverage." Dr. Kucinski opened a small refrigerator near his desk. "I'm afraid all I have to offer you is something non-alcoholic."

"As long as it's cold. By the way, I've been sober for almost two years now."

"Congratulations, Detective. That's only beneficial for your health."

"That's what my heart doctor says. I guess he knows what he's talking about."

Dr. Kucinski returned with two bottles of tea. He extended the bottles to John. "Flavored or unflavored?"

John looked at the labels on the bottles. "I'll take the unflavored. I never cared much for passion fruit."

Dr. Kucinski opened his bottle of tea and took his seat next to John. The two of them sat there drinking their tea for awhile. They watched the rush hour traffic on the busy street below them.

"Detective, it's obvious that these cases have haunted you for many years now. What are your thoughts and feelings now that you have retired? Do you feel remorse or some sort of personal responsibility?"

John nodded. "I should have done a better job of convincing my boss and the prosecutor's office that we had a serial killer. I think I could have done more to help those families out. In my mind I could see the day when I could tell them we caught the guy who ended the lives of those two women."

"Your superiors were evidently not as astute as you were, Detective. If they had been perhaps the investigations would have been more fruitful."

"Now, that right there means a lot to me, Doctor. The fact that a man with your knowledge would say that I was right in believing those cases were serial murders gives me, encouragement."

"You have researched the subject enough to know serial murderers do not always commit their acts in the same matter. Their motivations can often vary."

"From the cases I looked at I was pretty much able to rule out robbery, sexual assault, and even someone trying to get attention." John again looked at Dr. Kucinski to see if he was taking any notes. "You're more of an expert than I'll ever be. Let me ask you what you think about my profile of this person?"

Dr. Kucinski set his notepad next to his tea on the small round table between the recliners. "I believe you're an astute investigator as I said earlier. You were far more valuable then your superiors realized."

John finished his tea and set it down next to Dr. Kucinski's notepad. "I appreciate that. You know, I wished I would have had your help on those cases back then. Who knows, maybe we could have solved them?"

"*Who knows*?" Dr. Kucinski replied.

They sat and looked at the city for a few minutes. Neither of them said anything. The shadows from the buildings were longer now. It would not be long before the sun would set.

"I think he's still out there. I don't think he's ever stopped killing. He can't stop. He's probably still traveling around killing prostitutes or homeless people."

Dr. Kucinski cleared his throat. "I rather doubt this type of individual would stoop to such a manner. I would tend to think his preference would be the ordinary citizen."

John noticed that the sun had set and the street lights below were now lit.

"Well, Doctor, I'm glad I came here. Just talking with you has helped a lot. I guess I better be going. I've got about an hour drive ahead of me and I'm sure you need to get home to those grandkids. When can I talk to you..."

A peculiar look came across John's face. It was almost if he had seen something disturbing.

"Doctor, you're gonna think this is weird, but I can't get out of this chair."

Dr. Kucinski laughed. "Now, Detective, I warned you that this was the most comfortable chair you would ever sit in. I told you that I've had clients fall asleep in them and...."

"*No,*" John interrupted. "I'm trying to tell you I can't get up. I can't move. *Something's not right.*"

Dr. Kucinski rose quickly from his recliner. He proceeded to check John's feet and arms. John could barely feel the doctor's touch. Dr. Kucinski plopped back in the recliner and said, "Hmm. That's quite interesting."

"Well, what's *happening* to me?" John asked frantically. "Am I having a stroke or something? I think I'm paralyzed."

Dr. Kucinski leaned forward and patted John near his knee. "Oh, I forgot, you're unable to feel that aren't you?"

John shook his head and closed his eyes tightly.

"No, you're not having a stroke. Paralysis? Yes, that would be a more appropriate term."

"Well, can you call a doctor? I need help."

"Call for help? Absolutely, Detective. I'll arrange for an ambulance, but only after you listen to *my* story. It's only fair, don't you think? We in the mental health field need our therapy sessions as well."

John began to breathe rapidly and beads of sweat gathered on his forehead.

"Are you familiar with chemistry, or pharmacology?

"No," John grunted. "Would you please call for help?"

"Well, I've made quite a study of it," Dr. Kucinski continued. "What you're experiencing, Detective Denton, is what I like to call 'The Paralyzer'. He smiled. "It's something I've perfected over a number of years. I'm really impressed with myself at the risk of too much bravado."

"What did you do to me?" John strained.

"Well, you've seemed to have lost your astute ability. I'm *murdering* you, Detective." He checked his watch. "The Paralyzer affects your large voluntary muscles first and then the involuntary. Eventually your heart will stop. In approximately twenty minutes I shall place an emergency phone call about my client who is having chest pains in my office. When the EMT's arrive they will find me administering CPR to your lifeless body. With your history of heart disease the emergency room doctor will suspect heart failure. Even if they bother with an autopsy, which I rather doubt with their workload, the medical examiner will notice the deterioration in your heart structure. Not to mention your clogged arteries. You really should have taken better care of yourself. No, the Paralyzer is undetectable. I know the medical examiner quite well. The toxicology lab has failed to find it in five autopsies so far."

"So, you killed those two ladies in San Patricio?"

"Yes, I remember it so vividly. It was such a quaint little town you lived in. It was, so innocent."

"Glad you liked it."

"Do excuse my enthusiasm. You don't know how long I've wanted to talk with one of the investigators from one of my little adventures. I've also never been able to witness the complete effects of the Paralyzer."

"And of all the people I could have gone to I had to walk into your office."

"*Yes*! Look what fate hath brought?" Dr. Kucinski checked his watch. "You've got about fifteen minutes to conduct your interrogation of the suspect, Detective."

John found it difficult to speak, but managed to mumble. "Emily Johnson. Why her?"

"The young woman with the auburn hair? I believe you said she was a nurse?"

John moaned.

"Now that was a spur of a moment type of thing. She sat across from me on the plane from Denver back here to San Francisco." Dr. Kucinski made a face of disgust. "She had this box of greasy fried chicken that she was eating. The vile smacking sounds from this woman as she stuffed her face in front of us. All the passengers were annoyed by her."

"So you killed her for bad table manners?" John managed to get out.

"Partly. What caused my final decision was the fact that this woman licked her fingers. She licked each one over and over. Can you imagine the *germs*? When we retrieved our luggage from the baggage carousel I made sure to help her remove her bag. The address was there in plain site on the bag, so I drove to San Patricio and paid her a visit the next evening and took her to a lake nearby. She *licked* her fingers, so I removed them."

"Nobody but our department knew about the fingers missing. We thought the killer did that to hide her identity."

"Oh *please*, Detective. You're much better than that. If I had wanted to conceal her identity I would have removed her teeth as well."

"And Rebecca Owens, what about her?"

"The older lady? No reason in particular. I liked your town, so I decided to return. She was convenient."

"You have a daughter."

"Detective, if you're trying to lay a guilt trip on me it will be ineffective. Yes, I have a daughter *and* granddaughters. My choice of entertainment is entirely separate from my home life. You couldn't come close to understanding my mind."

"Why did you do it? Why kill all those people? I could never figure out your motivation."

"So that is why you attended my workshop on the motivation of serial murderers? You were hoping to find the answer?"

The room seemed to become more and dimmer for John. Dr. Kucinski's voice echoed and John could barely breathe now.

"Detective? Stay with me for a moment longer. Weren't you taking notes at my workshop? You know there is no one particular motivation. I would never place myself with those so called serial killers. What did you expect of me? To go out and kill prostitutes? To taunt the police and media with cryptic letters? How *cliché*"

Dr. Kucinski leaned over and spoke directly in John's ear.

"No, I never discriminated in whom I chose. Yes, Detective, it was me doing the killings in those cities. I had annual symposiums there, you know. I'd return for another one the following year and would see the need for entertainment. You ask a pertinent question, so I will give you my most succinct answer. I did it because I *wanted* to."

Dr. Kucinski grabbed John's wrist and felt a very faint pulse. He grabbed the bottles of tea and locked them in a file cabinet.

"I've really enjoyed talking with you. I must tell you that I never had the intention of killing you today, but such is fate." He again checked John's pulse. He was gone. "It looks as though this will be your final case, Detective. You were right about one thing; I'll never stop." Kucinski paused for a moment and looked closely at John's face. "Hmm, you almost look as though you're smiling. If you'll excuse me I'll be making that phone call now. I'll let the EMT's find you just right where you're at."

## MR. BARROW'S PERFECT MATCH

It was four thirty in the afternoon and an anxious Lindsay Reynolds skidded as she pulled into the parking space in front of Barrow's Computer Repair. She hurried inside. There was nobody in the store. Nobody at the counter.

"Hello?" she yelled. "I need some help out here."

"I'm coming," said a voice from the back room.

Mr. Barrow, the owner of the repair shop, stepped through the back room doorway and closed the door.

"Mr. Barrow? Is my computer ready? It's supposed to be ready. Reynolds? That's the name it's under."

Mr. Barrow scrutinized the young woman's face. Yeah, Reynolds, uh..."

"*Lindsay Reynolds*," she interjected.

"That's right," Mr. Barrow said as he nodded his head. "How's your daddy?"

Lindsay took a deep breath. "He's fine. My computer? I've come to pick up my computer. David said he'd have it fixed today. Is he here? Can you ask him?"

"David's not here. Everyone is gone. I always let everybody go home early on Fridays. Let me check and see if he fixed it." Mr. Barrow looked over the computers that were on the shelves marked 'Pickup'. "Nope, don't see it. Let's have a look over here...oh, OK, here it is, Reynolds, L." Mr. Barrow turned and frowned at Lindsay. "David told you it would be ready *today*?"

Lindsay nodded rapidly.

"I'm sorry, but it looks like he didn't get to it. The new part's sitting right on top of it though. I don't know why he didn't go ahead and install it. I'll have a talk with that boy. You can pick it up on..."

"*Please!*" Lindsay said almost in tears. "I have to have my computer. I need to use the app on it for a report. My boss needs it for court on Monday morning and nobody I called could open the office over the weekend."

Mr. Barrow nodded. "All right, all right. If you don't mind waiting I can fix it for you right now."

Lindsay pulled up a stool and sat down at the counter in front of Mr. Barrow.

Mr. Barrow looked around the counter and finally found a screwdriver. He began opening the case of the computer.

"Yes sir, we'll get you fixed up in just a little while," he said with a smile. "I remember this computer. I built it for you when you went to college."

Lindsay nodded.

"I guess you're out of college now?"

"Yes," Lindsay said as she stared at the counter top. "I'm a paralegal."

"A paralegal, huh? That's a good job. I remember when you were just a kid and you'd come in here with your brother to buy games. Course, now everybody downloads them. Your family sure has been good customers."

Mr. Barrow looked up from his work and noticed a tear running down Lindsay's cheek.

"Hmm, looks like it's more than just that report that's bothering you."

Lindsay sighed heavily and nodded.

"Well, maybe you ought to tell me about it seeing how I've known you and your family for so long now."

"It's just my emotions, Mr. Barrow. You wouldn't understand."

"What do you mean I wouldn't understand?" he asked. "Just because I work with machines doesn't mean that *I'm* one."

Lindsay continued to stare at the table.

"I just broke up with someone. I met him during my vacation. He's a legal aide in another state." Lindsay sighed heavily again and continued. "Sometimes I wish I had never met him. I don't want to ever get involved again. My emotions can't handle it. I loved him too much. I wanted him all the time, but I couldn't function because it's just too overwhelming." She wiped the tear off of her cheek. "You know, I was happy before I met him. I feel like the relationship and the intensity of it drove me crazy." She shook her head and laughed. "We were so much alike. Sometimes I feel like I should have become a nun or something. I don't even know why I'm telling you this." Lindsay looked up at Mr. Barrow. "Do you know what it's like to have something like that and lose it?"

Mr. Barrow put down the screwdriver and looked very intensely into Lindsay's eyes for a moment.

"I might know a little bit about that. I know about loving somebody you can never have." Barrow waited until he knew he had Lindsay's attention before continuing with his repairs. "When I was in my twenties and early thirties I always had trouble attracting women. Sure, they liked me and thought I was cute, but they never took me seriously. I went through my life and encountered many desirable women, but I almost never acted upon my impulses, and seldom introduced myself. When I did, I usually got the, '*Excuse me?*' response. So this just reinforced things. Of course I was never approached either. And so most of my friends had wives and I never even had dates." Mr. Barrow again glanced at Lindsay. She was no longer crying and seemed intensely interested in what he was saying. He continued on. "Well, I got interested in singles' ads on the Internet. God, that's been quite a few years now. Back then I thought American women were superficial and I was fed up with them. A lot of the women I knew acted like men, and frankly, I was rarely impressed with any of them. I began a fascination with the singles' ads from Russian and Ukrainian women. Here were beautiful women with traditional values and shy personalities. They valued and held men in high regard. It was perfect. I spent hours just looking at the photos and the personalities. Although I was too reserved to place an ad in a regular newspaper, I found the Internet to be ideal for me. My profile was available to the women from the countries surrounding Russia. I found it so sad that many of the photos contained the women's children. These women were willing to leave everything behind to start a new life with American men. So I got my first email with a photo. I felt great. I told everybody I knew about my new Ukrainian friend. I know it sounds silly, but I actually imagined what it would be like to be married to her. I imagined myself announcing to my friends and coworkers about how the Internet had brought two people together from so far away. Needless to say, she didn't write me back. I was disappointed, but there were others. I got my confidence up and began writing the women in the ads. I never got any responses. I think the women had to pay for each email they got. The companies that these women paid money to also weeded out many of the responses. This went on for about seven months or so. I started getting emails from women in this country and even locally. I wrote back and forth to a couple of very nice ladies from right here in town. They both stopped writing when I asked them for a photo. At that time I worked downtown in the bank plaza for First Mortgage. Back then I was the only computer technician they had. Now they have four full-time technicians and still can't keep up. I know because we get a lot of their repair work. Anyway, there were a lot of women working there. Most of the women were married and often tried to find me a wife. Not a girlfriend, mind you, but a *wife*. Nothing ever worked out. I was beginning to want to give up on my Internet ads. There were so many more men than women on the Internet that I found it almost impossible to compete. I tried the honest approach in my ad, but that didn't work. I even embellished a little and that still didn't do any good. I even went as far as to say, 'Email me and find out for yourself what I'm like.' I thought I did everything right including displaying a very nice photo of myself. I just couldn't get a chance."

Mr. Barrow again looked up from his work at Lindsay and smiled. His eyes seemed to suddenly have a sparkle to them.

"Then I met *her*. Her name was Jennifer Benkendorfer. Say that three times real fast." Mr. Barrow laughed and then continued working on the computer. "By accident I found this new website where she had placed an ad. As I said, I had been considering giving up my ads, but for some reason I went ahead and placed an ad of my own. As was my rule, I specifically stated in my ad that I would only deal with women who had photos of themselves available for me to see. During the time I had my ad on this service I got three responses. One was from a much older woman in Ukraine, another from a very tall woman in college who didn't write back to me, and one from Jennifer. She didn't have a photo of herself and she was an American. For some reason I decided to read about her personality. By then I had read hundreds of profiles, but none were like hers. It was almost as if somebody who knew me very well had written her ad. She described herself as shy and practical. There was no air of superficiality about her. What she wanted in a man was me one hundred per cent. She worked as a computer programmer in a small city about five hundred miles away. It all just hit me. I knew right then that this was incredibly special." Mr. Barrow paused and stared into space for a moment before continuing his train of thought. "You know, before this I always told my friends and coworkers about the emails I had gotten from the women, but I kept this one a secret. I guess I didn't want to jinx it. I wrote Jennifer right away. I took a chance and told her all about my personality, my lifestyle, and my job. I expected no reply, but I got one. She actually agreed with many of the things I had said. The things she wrote just amazed me because it was like having my mind read."

Mr. Barrow carefully unwrapped the plastic packaging from the new computer part. He started smiling.

"I was a bit of a songwriter in those days. I was pretty good, but I kept the songs to myself. I had hoped to have my songs published someday and I was moving towards that. Jennifer liked music and so I sent her a couple of songs that I had written using my computer. She really was impressed with them. So we continued writing almost daily. It was such an anticipation each time I checked my email. I felt terrible whenever I didn't receive any messages from her. Each email from her brought up thoughts of, 'God, this is unreal. There's somebody that thinks like I do. There's somebody that really likes me.' Here I was competing with no telling how many men and *I* was the one getting through. I still kept my personal ad active and I would occasionally look at ads. I really started paying attention to the personalities of the profiles that I read. None compared to Jennifer. Gradually, I lost interest in looking at the profiles. I began thinking of Jennifer more and more. For the first time it didn't really matter so much what the woman looked like. I was interested in her soul, not the shell. As I thought of her the question began popping up, 'What do I do? What do I *do*?'"

Mr. Barrow was finished with his repairs. He put his tools down and leaned on the counter towards Lindsay. She quickly glanced out the window and scanned the parking lot for cars. She hoped nobody would walk into the store and interrupt the story that she was so intensely interested in.

"So we went on sending messages back and forth for three months or so. We'd tell each other about our day and she would ask what songs I was working on. Every now and then she would have a problem with the computer she programmed on and I'd give her technical advice. While I was at work I would often wonder what she was thinking. Was she thinking the same things as me? Did she just like me, or was it more? Every once in awhile in a sentence or two we'd convey how we felt. We just communicated really well. I would get scared when she'd say something that I felt or when she described me to a T."

Mr. Barrow sighed.

"And so I imagined what it would be like to be with her. To live with her. To play my music for her and let her critique it. She dominated my thoughts in quiet moments. I spent more time writing messages to her than writing songs. Gosh, I spent so much time just daydreaming about her. Of course, I would be plagued with that same question, 'What do I do?' As the emotions became more intense the most powerful question popped into my head, 'What's the point?' I mean, here she was so far away and very happy and secure in her life. She had real opportunities with the company she worked for. I was happy as well. I had a meaningful life and my family was nearby."

Mr. Barrow finally pulled a stool over next to Lindsay and sat down. He rested his elbows on the counter.

"You know, the Russian women in the ads *wanted* to leave their lives to come to the great America. They never expected any of the American men to move to Russia. I had never thought about meeting an American woman. Writing emails to the women in all those ads was easy because I was so used to being turned down. I had no intention of moving and I certainly didn't expect Jennifer to ever uproot her life. I really had never thought of this. So, that was my predicament. We were so great, but what was the point? I had my life and she had hers." Mr. Barrow shook his head. "It was such a shame. It was as if somebody said, 'O.K., order up your perfect match.' Everything about her matched my preferences. The way she described herself matched what I liked to call my Dream Girl. She held me in high regard. I was scared because I was not used to this. In my history this had never happened. Beautiful and intelligent women never paid any attention to me. It was not reality. I became suspicious. I asked myself, 'Could it be a friend doing this? Could somebody be making up a fictional woman? Was she really a much older woman or one that I would not find attractive?"

"She could have been married," Lindsay interrupted.

"Hmm? *Yes*, she could have been married; *that's right*. Whether she was gorgeous, unattractive or a liar it just didn't matter because what was the point? Then I had a lot of negative thoughts. I started to think that maybe she deserved somebody better than me. I've gained about forty pounds since then, but look at me, here I was short and thin. I had a good job that I greatly loved, but it wasn't a high *paying* job. Then there was my freedom and privacy that I valued so much. Like you, my emotions were strong, but I didn't like having things complicated. I thought of the future and I really had overly negative thoughts. 'What if she divorced me? 'What if she was killed in an accident and I'd be left all alone?' All those stupid thoughts. So there I was. She had often talked of traveling here so she could visit me. As I said, I couldn't believe what was happening. Someone so wonderful and beautiful that was interested in *me*? I just *had* to know if she was real. I wanted to know if I would be as attracted to her physically as I was emotionally. We agreed on a plan and I sent her a one-way ticket to fly here. She would pay for the return. She told me how scared she was. I was really nervous too. I thought about how awkward it would be if we didn't click or if one of us was not attracted to the other. After I mailed her the ticket I actually felt calm, but she was still worried. Two days before she was to arrive I was mailed the ticket I had bought her. In the back of my mind I had figured this might happen. I received a lengthy email from her that evening. She apologized over and over, but told me that she just couldn't do it. She spoke of her life, her job, her house, her nearby family. She was really happy. She wanted to be with me, and she wanted to stay, but just like me, she also valued her life of privacy and solitude." Mr. Barrow looked down for a moment. "We were *too* much alike. It was a cruel twist of fate."

Mr. Barrow turned around and looked at the clock. He sighed heavily and turned back to Lindsay.

"I just stared at the walls that whole night. I had found what I had always been looking for and we couldn't be together."

"So what did you do?" Lindsay asked.

"I wrote a song for her. I worked on that thing just about an entire weekend. The lyrics were like I was handing over part of my soul to her." Mr. Barrow sighed heavily again. "So, it all ended."

"You mean you never met her?" asked Lindsay.

"Nope."

"You never even spoke to her on the phone?"

Mr. Barrow shook his head.

"Why didn't the two of you try and work something out?

"Well, what kind of relationship is that where you see each other once or twice a month? Maybe celebrities can do it, but not me. Saying goodbye so many times would have been too hard."

"You never wrote to Jennifer, or heard from her again?

Mr. Barrow nodded his head.

"Yeah. About a month later she mailed me a photo of herself. As soon as I looked at the photo I was hit with the same feeling as when I first read about her personality. Physically, she matched the dream girl that I've had in my imagination since I was a boy."

"So you *never* met each other?"

"*No*, Lindsay. I never heard the sound of her voice. I never looked into her eyes. Never smelled what kind of perfume she wore. Never caressed her skin with my fingers." Mr. Barrow's eyes began to water. "Most people would say it's crazy that two people who never met could experience so much. It was *real*, I tell you. It was on a much higher level because it wasn't based upon the physical. More passed between us than some couples who have been together for a long time."

Lindsay began to cry.

"What did you do?" she sobbed.

"I poured myself into songwriting. After that, I had the most productive sessions in my life. I tell you what; I even *sold* some of my songs. They even used one of my songs in a movie." Mr. Barrow laughed. "Now, don't ask which movie cause, believe me, you've never heard of it."

Lindsay smiled and wiped the tears from her eyes.

"What about the song you wrote for her?"

Immediately, the smile left Mr. Barrow's face.

"I burned the pages I wrote the lyrics on and I erased the music from my computer. You know, I play my music a lot for my friends and family, but I never play that one. In fact, I've *never* played it since." Again he sighed and gave Lindsay a tight smile. "So, I started working on the side repairing computers until I had too much work to handle. I opened up a shop of my own and eventually expanded to what you see here. I've got *five* people working for me.

"Well, don't you wonder what happened to Jennifer?" Lindsay asked.

"Of course I do. I think about her from time to time. I told you that I never played Jennifer's song, but I hear it in my mind every now and then. Jennifer used to create computer art and send them to me with her emails. I've got an old Pentium computer in the back and I fire it up every now and then when nobody's around so I can look at that art. That computer actually has a real keyboard, not the virtual keyboards that they have now."

"Do you look at the photo she sent you too?"

"No. I waited about six months before I looked at it again. It was too painful so I put it away and I haven't looked at it since. So, that's about it."

"God, Mr. Barrow; I never knew. Thank you so much for sharing all this with me."

Mr. Barrow smiled.

"Well, I think you needed to hear it, Lindsay." He knocked on the case of the computer. "Well, it's fixed. That'll be one hundred fifty for the part. They'll be no charge for the labor."

After Lindsay paid for the repair, Mr. Barrow picked up the computer and started carrying it out to Lindsay's car. Lindsay held the door for Mr. Barrow.

"You sure are different from others your age," Lindsay told him. "They think being single is so terrible."

"*Sure* they do," Mr. Barrow answered.

"There are a lot of people who never marry and I don't mean priests or nuns."

"Of course," Mr. Barrow said as he nodded. "There are lots of people who have no business being married."

"Right." Lindsay said as she retrieved her car keys from her purse. "What's so terrible about it?

"*Nothing*. Not one thing. Lindsay, there's nothing wrong with living alone as long as you're not totally alone and separated from society."

"Married people have so many problems," she said.

"How many arguments does a single person get into at home?" Mr. Barrow countered.

Lindsay smiled. "Yes, you *understand*." Lindsay opened her car door for Mr. Barrow.

"St. Paul himself said that it's better for people not to marry," Mr. Barrow said as he put the computer on the back seat. He then held the car door open for Lindsay. "Say hello to your daddy for me."

Lindsay got into her car and started the engine. She put down her window.

"I'm gonna be all right, Mr. Barrow."

"*Sure* you will."

"You've got the right idea, Mr. Barrow," Lindsay said as she began backing out of the parking space. "No wonder you're so happy all the time."

"*I've* got the right idea? Well, maybe, but life's full of surprises." Mr. Barrow checked his watch. "I got to close up shop and get home. I have to start dinner. It's my turn to cook... for my *wife*."

"*Mr. Barrow*! Lindsay shouted as she slammed on her brakes.

Mr. Barrow laughed loudly.

"Next time you come in I guess I'll have to tell you about *that* story."

*Author's Note:*

*I'd like to share the inspirations for the stories in Destiny Binds Us All.*

*The Therapist and the Panther: If Dan's situation with the therapist and the panther seems like a nightmare; it's because it is. I got the idea from a nightmare I had. The story is pretty much the same as the dream except that the therapist chastised the main character for voting for Ronald Reagan's re-election.*

*Paul vs. Jack: The idea also came from a dream. Although the situation is serious, the story is meant to be somewhat of a comedy. I remember waking up laughing. I particularly remember the line, "He's freakin' older than you, man."*

*Case of Fate: This story could very much have been a nightmare, but the idea actually came from my own imagination.*

*Mr. Barrow's Perfect Match: Now the idea for this little story came from neither a dream nor my imagination. It is pretty much autobiographical. Unlike Mr. Barrow, the woman I met left her job and family behind to be with me. We've been married ever since.*

Thank you for purchasing my book of stories. Please do me the favor of leaving your review of the book on the website you ordered it from. Also, be sure to check out my website for other books I have written, as well as titles I'm currently working on.

**henickebooks.com**

From my imagination to yours,

**Gary Henicke**